Sweet Girl

JACK WHITNEY

For my main bitch, Kay

Because this short literally would not
have been possible without you.

Thank you for bringing these two into my
life, and for always pushing me out of my
comfort zone and into terrifying places.

Chapter One
Gavin

"Hey, Gav." A decorator chucked a small package in my direction. "This was left at the office."

I caught the wrapped box just as the bartender slid a sample of one of the signature drinks for the singles event that night toward me— a pomegranate martini. I took a sip as I read the note on the gift.

Try to behave tonight.

Fucking Styx. I recognized the handwriting—had stared at it on gifts and packages for more than a few millennia, though in this millennia, it was mainly on Valentine's Day. Of course, this gift was no different. It was from my *dear* mother. Probably something boring accompanied by a card with instructions to keep my usual mischievous pranks to a minimum, to try not to piss off any more gods than I already had. Though, what was the fun in that?

I tossed the box over my shoulder and into the trash.

"What do you think?" the bartender asked me about the drink.

I took another sip of the sweetened beverage and gave her a nod. "Keep these coming to me later."

It was Valentine's Day, my favorite day of the year. I loved this holiday—*reveled* in everything that it was. After all, the day did feature me on all its marketing ploys and schemes. The old depiction of a cherub holding a bow and arrow seemed to be the favorite. They always got the drawings wrong. No matter how many painters I'd posed for before with suggestions on my true nature, most seemed to like the idea of a small boy, not a grown man.

Imagine the god of desire, a cherub…

I almost rolled my eyes just thinking about it.

I'd grown away from that over the last few decades— from striking strangers with arrows to toy with their emotions, usually in my godly form. Now, I used something much more potent to play games with: a dating app I'd created called Cupid's Arrow.

Gods, did I love playing with this app. It was so much easier than the old way of doing things.

My phone buzzed in my hand. Another RSVP had been claimed.

Perfect.

I chuckled under my breath at the triumph and pushed my phone into my back pocket, looking up just in time to see the banner for the party being strung across the ceiling.

As if everyone attending the party wasn't fully aware of the dating app sponsoring it.

"Hey, Av," I called out to my marketing coordinator.

Avril was standing across the bar room, instructing the two on the bar top whether to go up or down with the banner. She was fantastic at her job and one of my favorite people at the company; a middle-aged woman who actually bantered with me without taking it too seriously. She was always game for any wild ideas I might have.

"Yes, Cupid?" she called back. "You know, you don't have to be here," she added.

Every time someone used the name, I had to laugh. No one knew that I was truly Cupid. *Eros.* The god himself. They all thought they were clever when they gave me the nickname after I'd come up with the elaborate dating app years back.

It was fucking adorable.

Hands in my pockets, I made my way through the sea of tables and chairs to stand by Avril's side. As I considered the banner again, I reached for a dish of the naughty candy hearts we'd made for the event, then popped one that read 'DTF' into my mouth.

"A little up on the left—Sarah, was that a little, really?" Avril was saying.

"Do you think anyone will guess who's sponsoring the party?" I asked her in a low tone.

Avril glared sideways, her neck craning as she looked up at me from her short stature. "You hate it."

I popped another heart back. "A little ostentatious," I said, the corner of my lip lifting just so.

Avril stared at me as though she was ready to punch my face in, and I couldn't help giving her a crooked smirk, knowing the dimple beneath my short ginger scruff would reveal itself. Her lips twisted at the sight, and she huffed.

"It's a good thing you're cute," she muttered. "Take it down!" Avril announced, and the entire room stood still. But Avril was already gathering up some of the more obnoxious decorations. "Scale it back by half," she added, her brow raising at me as she snatched up things left and right into a rolling trash bin.

She grabbed one of the bowls of candy hearts, and I grabbed her wrist before she could toss it.

"Those stay," I said.

Frustration slipped from her expression, and a smile lifted in her eyes instead. "Oh, he likes the naughty hearts," she teased.

"Could be fun," I mused before picking up another.

GOOD GIRL, it read.

Avril chuckled softly as she crumbled up one of the heart papers. "The god has spoken," she said loudly to the decorating crew. "Leave the candies, the roses, and the confetti on the tables. Toss the rest."

I held Avril's—only slightly annoyed—gaze a moment, then slid a candy heart in her direction. She read it with knitted brows, nearly rolling her eyes, but unable to stifle her widening grin.

I winked at her before turning on my heel. "See you in an hour, Av," I told her. A few steps later, I circled, walking backward and saying, "You should wear something more fitting on those curves. Show off that body we all know you're hiding under there."

"There will be enough of that to go around tonight," she said. "Wait—you can't leave yet," she added urgently, having apparently realized I was heading out.

I frowned, but even as I started to reply, the back kitchen door swung open, and two of my co-workers came out with a small cake, sparklers erupting, and the number five drawn on in red atop the white icing.

Five years since the app's launch.

Claps sounded, and I laughed as a few of my friends and colleagues appeared to congratulate me. I wavered through the throng, running my hand through my fluffy ginger hair and over my face. I stopped to give them hugs, not daring to take all the credit as we'd only made it to five years due to their hard work. I couldn't have done it without this group. They were the core of the app's magic, why it thrived and attracted so many. I maneuvered through until I reached Avril, and then she handed me a gift.

"You really didn't have to," I said, pulling on the red velvet ribbon wrapped around the box. I had no idea what she or the rest of this group would have gotten, but it had to be one of two things: something wholly inappropriate or a gag gift.

"What is it? Did you—"

Red, fuzzy handcuffs fell into my hand.

Of fucking course.

I lifted a coy brow to Avril's satisfied smirk as whistles sounded from the rest of the crowd.

"Trying to tell me something, Av?" I asked.

"I think I speak for everyone when I say we hope you find someone to use them on tonight," she replied, and some people clapped heartily while a few others grabbed me by the shoulders, shaking me in a ragging manner. I couldn't stifle a wide grin as I stuffed the handcuffs in my back pocket.

My phone buzzed again—over a thousand invitations claimed.

"Alright, back to it—" I kissed Avril quickly on the cheek, then turned toward the door. "One hour until showtime."

Chapter Two
Chloe

One hour until I could go home.

That was how long I'd told my friend, Lana, I would stay at this singles party she was so desperate to attend. A singles party on Valentine's Day—typical. And, of course, it was being sponsored by the most popular dating app online right now, one that Lana was obsessed with and one that I hardly had time for. I barely had time to see my friends on the weekends, much less devote time and energy to strangers with bad pickup lines.

"It's not even a dating app," I had said a few hours earlier as I looked through my closet.

"Sure it is," Lana argued, standing in front of the mirror and checking out her ass in the fitted red dress she was wearing.

"Name one actual date you've ever been on using that app," I challenged.

"I went out with…" Lana paused, and I laughed.

"Exactly."

But Lana ignored me. "You can select what you're looking for," she argued. "Marriage, one-night hookup, casual, friends—"

"Someone to murder you," I muttered under my breath.

"Well," Lana turned and pulled a leather skirt from the closet, "if that's what you're into," she winked.

I adjusted the high-waisted, black leather mini-skirt Lana had chosen for me to wear as we waited in line outside the bar. A rogue snowstorm had come in that day, and the chill of it had me pulling my long coat tighter around my body.

I needed a drink.

"Do you have your invitation?" Lana asked. "You have to RSVP to get in."

I drew my phone out, fingers nearly numb with the cold as I fumbled onto the app to accept the local invite. A slew of notifications and messages popped up, but I ignored them. I could see Lana's playful smile out of the corner of my eye, and I gave her a sour look.

"What?" I asked.

"I knew you had the app," Lana grinned.

Guilty.

I had wandered onto it over Christmas just to see what the fuss was about, and honestly to find someone to distract me from family matters, preferably with equipment he knew how to use. Needless to say, after a dozen unsolicited dick pics, false promises, and one late-night coffee date too many, I'd deleted everything off the app except for my profile photo and turned notifications off.

We reached the door then. The bouncer gave us a quick, leering smile and once over before saying, "Enjoy, ladies," and he let us inside.

"Wait—I thought—"

Lana ignored me as she shrugged her leopard print coat off.

"You mean I didn't have to accept that stupid invitation?" I asked.

"Of course not," Lana laughed. "I honestly just wanted to see if you had an account."

I resisted a chuckle and shook my head at her. "You're such a bitch," I declared.

"You love me," Lana shrugged.

A smile slipped through my facade. I did. Lana had been there for me after I'd practically abandoned everyone else I knew, a time when I didn't know I needed saving. She'd forced her way by my side and refused to let me drown. And for that, I will forever be grateful.

Warmth finally hit my chilled cheeks as we moved further inside and away from the entrance. The place was packed already—smells of alcohol and candy filling the air as though it was being pumped in. I could hardly hear the music due to the noises of people laughing and chatting and their drinks clanking together. Lana found us a standing table, and the moment we reached it, I grabbed the drink menu. I needed alcohol in my shivering body as soon as humanly possible.

There were six signature cocktails for the night, and the names of a few caused me to laugh.

"Love Potion Number Nine," I named off, smirking at Lana. "Because why wouldn't you have a drink named that at a Valentine's party?"

"These are fun," Lana said as she reached into the bowl of candy hearts and drew one out. "CHOKE ME," she read. "Well, at least they're direct."

I took a handful of the hearts out and laid them on the table. It was certainly the most fun use of candy hearts I'd ever seen. "I like this one better," I said before pushing a heart in Lana's direction.

FUCK OFF, it read.

Lana laughed. "How many idiots do you think we can turn away tonight using only the candies?"

I lit up at the idea but was wary of Lana's true intentions.

"You're trying to get me to stay longer, aren't you?" I asked.

"Obviously."

I placed a heart on my tongue, making sure Lana saw the word 'BLOCKED' on it before curling it back into my mouth. Lana chuckled again, and I spotted the waitress making her way through the crowd toward us. She was carrying a few of the night's cocktails, and I chose a Scarlett Kiss while Lana chose a Love Potion.

"To finally getting you away from your computer," Lana said, raising her glass.

"To this hour going by quickly, so I can get out of these heels," I countered.

Lana arched a perfectly-trimmed, smug brow. "Someone will certainly be getting you out of those heels," she drawled. "Cheers to the one who does."

Chapter Three
Gavin

I chose a seat at the far end of the bar to watch the fun while chatting with a few friends from work. While the party started up, I'd made time to pull out the app and do a little dancing around with the profiles, nudging some people in the right direction for a strong connection and shifting a few I knew would be explosive in the end. Those were my favorites, the ones I was most proud of, and every now and then, they happened to work out. But most of the time, they were just fun to watch, and seeing them play out in real time there at the bar was set to be the highlight of my night.

Drinks were flowing. The music was a thudding white noise in the background to all the laughter and talking around the room. People were loving the candy hearts and matching on the app... Everything was going according to plan. It was all perfect... a *normal* Valentine's night...

Until she walked in.

Fuck me.

Everything my friend, Zayn, was saying, muted. The woman was shrugging her black trench coat off, revealing the off-shoulder light pink sweater tucked into a wide belt over her leather mini-skirt; her full, pillowed breasts pushed up and exposed along the vee neckline. Her long legs were hidden beneath a sheer layer of black tights and thigh-high black-heeled boots. Just the peek of those tights had me more curious about her, of whether she'd worn full tights or if they were connected to some slutty lingerie beneath.

Fucking gods, I hoped it was the latter.

The fantasy of her in something strappy, perhaps sprawled out on the bed, her wrists locked together over her head with my new fuzzy handcuffs, filled my mind. I already wanted to set those beautiful tits free, feel how soft they would be in my mouth, bracing my cheeks—

Shit, she'd barely been in the room for three minutes, and I was already plotting all the ways I would have her.

She laughed at something her friend said, then absentmindedly pushed her long, silky black hair off her face as she reached for the drink menu. Her smokey makeup accentuated her warm ivory skin and highlighted her round, dark eyes.

How fucking beautiful she would look on her knees... my hand threaded through her soft strands, those wide eyes looking up at me as she took my cock deep…

I shifted in my seat as the image stirred my now attentive dick. Where the fuck had she come from? She wasn't on any list of persons I knew would attend, nor did I remember her profile even showing up in this area of the country. She was a ghost. An apparition come to drive me toward insanity if I couldn't have her.

One of the neon red lights ricocheted off her friend's bouncing textured hair, caramel streaks in the tamed spirals, and bathed her light brown skin in its glare. The pair were looking at the candy hearts, and I couldn't fight my swallow as the girl I was admiring laid one on her tongue and rolled it back into her mouth.

Shit.

"Hey, Gav—" Zayn snapped his fingers in my face twice, and I zipped out of the daze.

I was a breath away from slapping the knowing grin off Zayn's face.

"She's cute," Zayn said, sipping his drink as he glanced her way.

"She is," I agreed. "I don't remember seeing her on my list."

"Open party," Zayn shrugged. "Sure, a few will slip in with friends."

Though, I did recognize her friend. I'd seen her profile many times before, had seen some of the people she'd matched with, and even had some fun of my own matching her with a few I thought could be interesting.

I took my phone out with a plan in mind. Time for some fun.

My friends continued to chat around me, but I couldn't stop stealing glances at the girl. I noticed a couple of guys coming up to chat and watched as the two women slid candy hearts in their direction. It didn't take me being at the table to know they were using hearts with rejection sayings on them. A few of the men looked pissed off while others laughed, seemingly intrigued by the game.

It had been a long time since I'd genuinely lusted after another. Most of the mortals I'd found myself in bed with had been last-minute suggestions, mere glances exchanged that ended up with my taking them home and fucking in the back of my Jeep Wrangler.

This woman… I had a feeling I might have to do more than smile to get her attention.

I'd start with the basics.

Chapter Four
Chloe

I slid a candy heart reading 'THANK U, NEXT' toward the latest man that had approached to buy me a drink. It wasn't even that he wasn't good-looking. I was simply having entirely too much fun with the game Lana and I were playing. Even the onlookers were having fun with it once they found out what we were doing. A few had come up to us just to see what hearts we would give them.

And for the first time in months, I actually forgot about work.

I practically felt my jaw unclench and my shoulders relax with every smile and laugh. I kept my phone face down on the table, and every time I thought about checking my email, I reached for a candy heart or took a sip of my drink instead.

Needless to say, I was definitely feeling the effects already.

Shots of candy vodka were passed out from the waitress, and Lana and I cheers'd again before shooting them back.

"So, have you seen him?" Lana asked, and I frowned at the vagueness of her question.

"Seen who?" I asked as I sorted through a few more of the candy hearts.

"The hot ginger guy in the corner that's been staring at you since we walked in," Lana explained, her drink hiding her lips.

I looked up from the bowl, eyes narrowing at Lana's attempt at being secretive. "You realize you look even more suspicious doing that, right?" I turned back to the hearts and shook my head. "In the corner… let me guess. He's hidden in the shadows with a *very* mysterious look about him."

"No, he's in full light," Lana countered. She hugged her drink closer, and I noted the leer in her gaze as she stared in his direction. "If you don't go talk to him, I will."

"Here you go," the waitress announced as she circled around, two more drinks on her tray—the pomegranate martinis I'd been eager to try.

"Wait," I stopped her, confused by the drinks landing on the table that we hadn't asked for. "We didn't order these."

"No," the waitress agreed, a smile splitting her red-painted lips. "But he did," she added with a nod to the man at the end of the bar—the ginger I assumed Lana had been talking about.

Well. At least Lana wasn't completely full of shit.

He was undoubtedly the sexiest thing at that party.

Fluffy, dark ginger hair, strong brows, a pointed chin... He was structurally god-like, and I wondered what exactly was wrong with him that he was at a singles party on Valentine's Day.

He was chatting with a few people who it looked like he knew. The deep dimple in his right cheek appeared with his crooked, flirtatious smile, that red scruff lining his jaw and upper lip at just the right length...

I took another slow sip of the sweet martini as I continued to look him over—noting the shadows of his strong shoulders creasing his cream-color sweater, his firm hand wrapping around his drink. He laughed, and his buddy shook his shoulder for a second, both regarding another friend who was animatedly saying something. My gaze skated back to his face, noticing his pale, freckle-dotted skin, now slightly illuminated by the flash of neon red from a spotlight swirling the room.

My bottom lip absentmindedly drew behind my teeth as I suddenly imagined the scruff on his jaw scratching against my inner thighs, tickling my flesh, that lopsided grin against my—

Stop, I told myself.

But *fuck*, I groaned inwardly. It had been entirely too long since I'd been thoroughly railed—just blatantly fucked like a dirty whore on New Year's. No expectations, no feelings. Just hard, toe-curling, mind-numbing, bruised in all the right places, sex.

God, I needed that.

I cursed myself for the imagery invading my mind and took another sip of my drink, intent on turning back to Lana to say something, but whatever I had in my mind wholly escaped me when my eyes lifted.

He was looking my way, and my heart skipped out of surprise.

His grin had softened, soft almond-shaped eyes holding my own, and his chin tilted just noticeably. The corner of his slightly agape mouth flinched almost like he would smirk, and he glanced down at his hands, tongue darting out over his lips before glancing in my direction once more, and this time… fucking hell. This time, that smirk appeared just faintly on his parted mouth. The way his eyes washed over me made me feel as though he meant to claim my entire being that night, perhaps even in this room behind some closet door where I would have to be gagged to stifle my moans while he bent to his knees beneath my skirt.

I couldn't control my shifting weight or tightening thighs. Heat spread on my cheeks, and I wasn't sure if it was from the way he stared or the strength of the drinks.

"Water," I blurted out before the waitress could leave the table. "Please."

The waitress snickered at me but nodded and turned to retrieve it.

"Look at that," Lana drawled, toying with the straw in her drink that she was still nursing. "We have a winner."

"I bet he's a prick," I said quickly, that heat on my face now spreading down my neck and across my chest. "Or doesn't know how to use his cock. Someone that pretty can't do it all."

"I have a feeling you're going to find out," Lana replied.

"Hi, ladies," a man announced as he and his friend approached. Handsome and with dark hair, I couldn't deny my attraction to them any more than I could with the other men that had approached. The one who had spoken was eyeing Lana as though he knew her, however, and I had to hide my grin behind my drink.

"It's Lana, right?" he asked.

Surprise lifted Lana's features. "Stalker status there, but yes, it is," she answered, intrigued.

The man held up his phone. "I saw we were matched, so I wanted to come say 'hi' instead of messaging since we were both here."

Lana frowned at the screen, and I snorted into my cup. "I don't… I haven't been online since we got here." Lana fumbled to take her own phone out and check it. A few notifications were there that hadn't been before, and Lana tapped to find new matches.

"Wow, I must be drunker than I thought," she muttered before laying the phone face down and turning her attention to him. "Adam?"

I tuned them out as I peered around the rest of the crowd, my eyes wandering first to the spot where the handsome ginger had sat, and my heart fell upon seeing he was no longer there. Of course. The first guy I found I might be willing to bring back to my apartment would disappear just to find someone easier.

It was a trend I'd grown accustomed to—attractive men acting as though they were interested in me from afar, always staring and sending a drink over, but never approaching. I usually saw them later chatting with other women and had often wondered what was wrong with me. Thankfully, I'd gotten so used to it that it rarely bothered me now. Their loss.

I blamed it on my resting bitch face that I'd come to love.

Adam's friend tried talking to me as Adam chatted up Lana. I barely caught the end of what he'd opened up with as friendly conversation. Something about the number of people that had shown up for the party. I attempted to engage for Lana's sake, seeing as she seemed to be enjoying herself, but I didn't give up my search around the room for my handsome stranger.

"Name is Chad," the friend said, and I didn't have to look at him to know he was wholly looking me over, his gaze lingering on my breasts as most men's usually did.

"It's always awkward, isn't it?" he added.

My attention staggered on him, slightly annoyed that he'd introduced himself and went on about the conversation as though he'd no interest in my own name and was rather thoroughly intrigued by my breasts alone.

However, I didn't blame him. They were great tits.

"What?" I asked as I looked away to continue my search.

"Being the wingman," Chad explained before downing his drink. "Third wheel. It makes me crazy."

Ex-fucking-scuse me.

My full attention diverted back. Another tick of annoyance soared through me as my fingers coiled around my martini glass. "You think I'm just here in case she decides she needs an excuse to leave early?" I snapped.

Chad considered me a moment as his throat bobbed with a swallow of his drink. "No need to get an attitude, princess," he said. "I'm here as his wingman, too."

"Princess…" I scoffed. I hated when someone called me that in such a condescending manner. "I suppose you think that by default, we'll be sharing some sort of night together where you claim to please me?"

"I've been known to take one for the team," he said, eyes dancing deliberately over me again. "Though with you, I think I might enjoy it."

"What makes you think I have any interest in you?"

He stepped closer. "You will."

"Will I?" This guy had to be fucking kidding me.

I set my drink on the table, hand resting on my hip as my chin raised challengingly. "Do you also think I'll enjoy the two pumps of your cock inside me before you get off?" I asked. "If you even make it there. From the looks of it, you're going to come in your pants staring at my tits. Are you enjoying the view? They are directly in your face, after all."

Chad stared at me, the leer that had been in his eyes now vacant. "You should watch that attitude of yours," he said, his voice stiffening. "Try being less of a bitch."

I choked out a sarcastic laugh. "Poor thing, I bet you thought that was an insult," I said with a tilt of my head.

"Princess, taking you home tonight would be an insult to my reputation," he shot.

I blinked and took a deep breath as I tried to stay calm. I reminded myself that I shouldn't drink whiskey. It usually brought out my fight response.

And I really wanted to punch this idiot in the face.

"Call me princess again, and the ambulance will be the one taking you home," I said through a clenched smile.

"There you are—"

The new, rasping voice raised the hair on the back of my neck. A large hand slithered around my waist, soft lips and scruff brushing my skin as the person leaned down and kissed my temple. The smell of peppered musk entered my nostrils—a sweet yet heated scent that enveloped my entire body like a warm, comforting blanket.

I didn't have to look over my shoulder to know it was the sexy ginger stranger from the other side of the room that had joined us.

And that damn smirk was staring at me when he practically skirted between myself and Chad.

"I've looked everywhere for you," he continued.

Sexy Ginger's gaze held mine as I inhaled deeply to calm myself, and I took a long sip of my drink before giving him a teasing smile. "I told you what I was wearing," I finally replied, playing along and nearly jumping him for saving me from knocking Chad on his ass.

"You told me what you were wearing beneath it," he replied, crooking a flirtatious brow, those eyes shifting over me in a way that made my cheeks red. I resisted chuckling at the comment and the leering gaze he stared at me with.

"Not this ensemble," he finished.

Oh, he was good.

And I could tell by the mischievous glint in his eyes that he fucking knew it too.

Chad cleared his throat, and Hot as Sin pushed off the table, pretending to have just noticed him standing there.

"Sorry, friend," Ginger said, giving Chad a clap on his shoulder. "I have blinders on when it comes to beautiful women. I didn't notice you there."

Chad's jaw clenched, and I noticed Sexy Ginger's fingers digging tighter and tighter around Chad's shoulder, almost like a warning. I could see Chad's expression faltering, pain stretching across his features as Ginger sunk his fingers deep into Chad's clavicle.

"I was just—"

"Finding someone else to bother?" Sexy Ginger suggested, his expression growing stern.

Heat pooled in my stomach. I shifted at the demand and brazen nature of the act, hating myself for how much it was turning me on.

Chad's hand clenched so tightly around his glass that I thought it might break. "I was just going to get a drink for my friend," he said through unmoving teeth.

Sexy released Chad's shoulder slowly, and then he did something that made my eyes widen.

He mockingly tapped Chad's cheek twice, and said, "Good boy," in a threateningly deep, sardonic tone that even sent a warning pulse all the way to *my* core.

Seeming to think the exchange was over, Sexy Ginger turned his attention back to me with a sigh and lift of that smirk on his lips… smiling as though he had successfully rid us of a pest. But I saw Chad's glaring face turn a deep shade of carmine, and I braced myself for what might come next. Chad set his drink on the table, his fists curling, and I knew the idiot was about to come at us.

I threw my full drink in Chad's face before he could make his move.

Whistles sounded around, and a few 'Ooo's' followed with laughter. Chad sputtered and wiped his eyes of the stinging alcohol, and I slammed my empty glass on the table.

"If you're going to hit someone, don't be a fucking coward and do it while their back is turned," I snapped.

"What—*the fuck happened, bro?!*"

Adam pushed between Sexy Ginger and I just as Lana grabbed my arm.

"Damn, Clo," Lana chuckled. "Hate to know what got that reaction. I need to bring you out more often. You're living all my dreams tonight."

A waitress came by then and pulled a rag from her apron. She handed it to Chad, and without saying a word to the idiot, she turned to me.

"New drink?" she asked, apparently amused by the scuffle.

"Please," I replied, and when I looked up, I couldn't stop my own smirk from rising on my lips.

Sexy Ginger was staring down at me, that crooked smile showing, his brows slightly narrowed as though he were still processing what had just happened.

"Now we're even," I said.

"I misread the room," he said, his hand clenching his chest. "Here I thought you were a damsel in need of saving. Turns out you're the fucking knight."

The waitress handed him a rag to wipe his face with as some of my drink had managed to splatter in his direction, and he gave her a nod. "Thank you, Wendy."

"No problem, Gav," she replied. "Another?"

"I think so," he said slowly, continuing to watch me with an intrigued stare.

However, my attention moved to Adam and Chad, who were still cleaning up, cursing us, and glowering at the onlookers who continued to laugh and snicker behind their backs.

"Isn't it always the thing with men?" I mused as I looked at my sexy stranger, head lifting triumphantly. "Showing off that testosterone and manly urge to claim and fight."

That damn dimple appeared on the right side of his angled grin as he reached into the bowl of candy hearts and proceeded to lay a few out on our table.

YOU'RE MINE

BE MINE

R U MINE

I'M YOURS

U R MINE

"Are you saying I should trash these, then, so they don't make our way into our game later?" he asked.

I could practically feel my eyes dilating at the mention of a game and naughty candy hearts. "I've never played that game."

"Don't worry. I'll teach you the rules," he said.

"Never really been a fan of those. I like to make my own."

He scoffed, his gaze traveling over me as he sucked his lip behind his teeth, oblivious he was in danger of falling for my charms and willingly debating his next move.

"Gavin," he introduced himself.

There was a name I could absolutely hear myself screaming later.

"Gavin…" I said his name slowly, letting it sit on my tongue for a moment, tasting it, imagining how it might sound as I moaned it while he tasted me, touched me…

I loved it.

"I'm Chloe," I said. "This is my friend, Lana."

Chloe.

I couldn't fucking wait to say that name later. Taste that name. Taste *her*. And after that scene, her throwing her drink in that guy's face?

Fuck me.

I was a heartbeat away from throwing her against the wall between the bathrooms and seeing just how wet her pussy was from the adrenaline. The way she was staring at me then, that devious, seducing glint in her eyes… it had my heartbeat picking up.

"You're not a serial killer, are you, Gavin?" her friend, Lana, interjected into the conversation. She leaned her elbows on the table, her slight cleavage pushing up between her arms. "—Actually, if you are, I hope she's the one who makes you change your ways. Helps you see the light." Lana winked at me, and I couldn't help my huff of amusement.

"And that's goodbye, Lana," Chloe said with a full, mocking smile. "Don't you have someone else to talk to?" she added with a nod to the man who had just sat his drink down on the table behind her. Lana grinned around the straw in her mouth, biting the plastic between her teeth, and she shifted her attention to her new friend.

Chloe shook her head as she turned back to me. "You're not a serial killer, are you?" she asked as the waitress sat our drinks down.

"What if I told you I was Cupid," I asked.

"Eros?" she said, brows raised.

"Whichever you prefer," I answered.

"Then I would say you're worse than a serial killer," she replied. "You make people fall in love."

"Love is death?"

"Love is unrealistic and tragic," she answered. "No matter how much you love someone or something, death will eventually take it away."

"Everyone loves something," I countered. "Shouldn't love be part of life's enjoyment? Otherwise, what's the point?"

She seemed to consider it, her short black nails tapping on the martini glass. "If you are Cupid, what are you doing here? Shouldn't you be flying around, shooting arrows in people's asses?"

I chuckled and resisted telling her I was fully capable of doing that with my phone now. "Taking the night off," I answered.

"Oh? Isn't this a popular night?"

"It's a bit cliche to fall in love on Valentine's Day, don't you think?" I said. "Besides, I've found something much more intriguing to spend my night with."

"What's that?" And the way her eyes dilated made a smile twitch at the corner of my mouth.

"You."

She stared at me a moment, her lips twisting in amusement, a soft glisten rising in her eyes like she was holding in laughter.

"Did you steal that from a romance novel?" she asked.

"Heard one of the other idiots at the end of the bar say it," I replied. "Thought I would see if it worked."

"Did it work for him?"

"It did not."

"Why would you think it would work on me, then?"

"You look like you read romance novels," I bantered. "I thought the line might spark your curiosity. Make you feel like you were in one—the filthy kind, of course."

"Sorry, you're not really my type in that genre," she said as she sat down her glass.

"What's your type?"

Her chin lifted, mockery dancing in her eyes. "Minotaurs," she answered.

Gods, she was fucking cute.

I settled my elbow against the wood and eyed the smug look on her face. She probably thought that word would send me running for the hills, but the joke was on her. I'd known a few minotaurs centuries back, ones that would have gladly taken her for a ride and given her exactly what those books promised.

Shame they'd since hidden themselves.

Chloe hadn't stopped smiling since I'd come over. Her confidence radiated with every rise and fall of her breasts, every twist of her finger in her hair, or lips wrapping around the straw in her drink. It had me wild for her, completely ignorant of the rest of the room, of the schemes I'd planned on playing with the guests here and the app, or of even what my next move would be. And the way her eyes glittered up at me?

Fucking Styx, I didn't know how long I could wait to have her.

"Here I thought you looked more like the faerie erotica type," I teased her.

She paused, evidently trying to keep herself from grinning outright as she twisted her red-stained lips, pulling her cheeks in and biting them. I stifled a groan as I imagined how those lips would pucker and plump around my cock, how that scarlet color would smear so beautifully around her mouth…

"You seem to know a lot about fantasy romance," she said, drawing me out of my trance.

"I'm Cupid," I said with a shrug. "It's part of my job to know these things."

There was a brief second when it looked like she genuinely considered the possibility. Her bright eyes squinted slightly, nails strumming on her glass again.

"Okay, *Cupid*," she said, saying my name like it was a joke. "Is that—"

A drunk man cut between us then, laughing as one of his friends had pushed him. Chloe jolted back, hugging her drink to her, but the new man seemed dazed and confused when he looked up and found her staring.

"I've fallen and found an angel," the man said.

I couldn't keep my soft laughter down. Chloe caught my eye as she rolled her own, and I reached into the bowl of candy hearts.

One of the friends shook the drunk man's shoulders as I stepped out from behind them. The three men were still gathering their wits, not paying attention to anyone else, and I took the opportunity to move to Chloe's side.

Brushing halfway in front of her, I held up the candy heart I'd chosen, letting her see it briefly and gaging the look in her eyes before tucking my finger delicately beneath her chin and bending to whisper, "Open wide," into her hair.

Pure lust rose in those shimmering eyes… lust that I intended to take advantage of in every way these naughty candy hearts told me to. Her lips parted just so, as I tilted her head back by her chin. I held her gaze hostage and placed that heart on her tongue, and for a second, it was all I could do to hold myself back from moving further… from skimming my thumb on her pouting scarlet lip, grazing my finger along her highlighted cheek, or curling my hand in her silky hair…

That white candy heart on her tongue was a siren's song to my crazed, immortal soul—calling me out on my insatiable desire for this woman… *this* woman…

I needed to consume her.

To touch her.

Taste her.

Feel her.

A whisper of my touch against her throat was the last thing I left her with before making my way back across the room.

Chapter Six
Chloe

The candy heart seemed to burn on my tongue. His touch was a brand I couldn't get out of my head. I could still feel his fingers on my chin, brushing my throat… My face and neck heated as I relived those last few moments over and over.

I remained in a stupor over the way his gruff whisper had made the hair on my neck rise until Lana finally pushed up behind me.

"That was *hot*," Lana said in a low tone, leaning eagerly on her elbows beside me. "God, that was hot. What did the heart say?"

I crushed the heart between my teeth and met Lana's eyes. "Be mine," I answered.

Lana slumped as though the words had made her weak. "Ugh. Fuck off, Clo," she said. "You go out one night and you find the hottest thing in the room, who also happens to be charming and not a complete dick. Where is this luck of mine?"

One of the men who came to join our table cleared his throat, and Lana stared at him.

"Too eager." She slid over a candy that read BOI BYE in his direction, but all he did was laugh.

I sipped on my water as Lana and the new man, David, began bantering back and forth. His friend, Devon, tried chatting with me, but it was all I could do not to try and find Gavin in the crowd.

My one-hour timer went off, and Lana raised a brow in my direction.

I hated giving Lana the satisfaction of being right, of admitting I wanted to stay longer.

However, I couldn't stop thinking about him.

Lana's face lit up as she watched me hit the 'dismiss' button, and then she threw her hands in the air with a loud cheer—going as far as to flag down the waitress for another round of candy vodka shots.

I shot back the liquid while flipping Lana off.

No matter how intriguing the conversation might have been with Lana and the three men laughing with her, I couldn't stop my wandering eyes.

It was almost as though his entire presence had been a fantasy.

Someone bumped into me a few minutes later, a hand sliding softly on my waist, and I swore I felt a finger dig into my belt. But the touch was gone within the second, and the person had fluttered back into the crowd by the time I managed to turn around.

There was something pressed beneath my belt.

I dug into it and bit my lips together upon seeing the candy heart.

HEY SEXY

I tried searching around the crowd without making it obvious, and eventually, I found Gavin's handsome face by the bar. I popped the candy into my mouth as we locked eyes, then deliberately rolled it back on my tongue.

He was so fucking cute.

He smiled crookedly at me, one hand shoving in his pockets as he turned back and pretended to laugh with his friends. He'd pushed the sleeves of his snug-fitting cream sweater up, revealing a few tattoos on those forearms—forearms that I wanted to see extended from my neck as he wrapped those long fingers around my throat. I eyed the firm grip he held on his drink, warmth pooling between my thighs at the vision of that grip on my ass or entwined in my hair…

A popular song came on the jukebox, and the entire bar erupted in cheers. I pulled myself out of the trance as Lana jumped up and down at my side, her arm punching the air. Lana grabbed one of the guys we were chatting with and dragged him closer to her. I laughed out loud as she attempted to dance with him, and, to my surprise, the man, David, kept up with her.

I nursed my cocktail as I stood back to watch and shake my head at Lana's terrible dancing. And when I looked over for Gavin, he was gone.

"Who knew this song could cause such a *distraction*."

Awareness stretched from my ears down my spine and between my legs at the sound of Gavin's voice. I hugged my arms tighter as I continued to watch Lana, though my mind stayed only on the hot magnetism of Gavin at my side.

David twirled Lana, making her hair bounce, and Lana's smile became so bright that it was like the entire room was suddenly her own stage.

I leaned a little closer to Gavin, our arms brushing. "It would be a perfect move of the hero in a romance novel to put this song on so that everyone was looking the other way just so he could swoon the heroine off her feet," I said before pivoting to face him.

"I agree," he said. "The hero would probably ask her to dance with him. Maybe tell her how beautiful she looked or how he admired her outfit."

"He'd be a gentleman about it, too," I added. "Sing a little to her. Offer to buy her another drink. Of course, he would keep his hands to himself and not do anything… *inappropriate*."

"Your hero sounds like an idiot," Gavin said.

I resisted a laugh and swirled my drink, suspicious of the devious smirk on his lips. "You didn't happen to turn on this song, did you?"

Gavin's deep chuckle made me shift. He took the drink from my hand and set both our glasses on the table at my back before pressing his hands into the edge on either side of my ribs, trapping me in his embrace. My breath hitched. Our bodies were nearly flush. His warmth blanketed me as my lashes lifted, and I watched his blown pupils travel over my face, eventually landing on my own, and I was paralyzed by the lustful glow emitting back at me from his eyes.

"Sweet girl, I'm not your hero," he rasped. "I'm the god of lust... *desire*... I'm the shadow you see in the dark when you think someone is watching you touch yourself, the blank face you see when you stare at the walls and imagine someone between your thighs. I'm the god you pray to when your thighs shake and your breaths cease... I'm *every* wicked fantasy you've ever had."

Oh, fucking hell.

I squeezed my thighs at the restless ache rising between them. "All of them?" I asked.

His chest pressed to mine, his head bending lower, and I found my gaze moving to his lips, my hands slightly grasping at his sweater. The soft thread and his stern chest burned beneath my fingertips as his next words hit my lips.

"Be mine tonight, and I'll show you."

The room erupted with more cheers. The song finished, and Gavin took a step back. That smile grew again as the darkened glow lifted from his green eyes.

Lana's laughter cut the blunt noise around us, bringing me back to reality as Lana and David nearly fell into the table. I shook my head at my friend, almost envious of the way her smile lit up a room.

And when I turned back to Gavin, he was gone.

I really wished he would stop disappearing like that.

I started to pick up my drink, only to find another candy heart on the table beside it.

R U WET

I wanted him to find out for himself.

My pussy pulsed at the fantasy. I could still smell his cologne lingering in the air. Still feel his breath on my lips as he'd spoken those words. I turned around, my head on a swivel as I looked for his hair, and finally I spotted him back with the friend he'd been chatting with most of the night.

I grabbed one of the hearts and made my way across the room, making sure to stay out of his sightline as I maneuvered through the crowd. When I reached him, I slid my hand in his back pocket, dropped the heart in securely, and then pushed past him toward the bathroom.

The white stalls were a hum of noise compared to the rowdy bar.

I paused at the first sink and pressed my hands into the porcelain. Thank fuck I'd been nursing that last martini and switching with water. I was glad I wasn't joining the other few girls in the stalls puking. I'd been there too many times before, woken up too many times with a headache from hell and craving water.

I met my gaze in the mirror, then groaned loudly at the sight. I was already a mess. I worked fast to revive my face and hair, reapplying the dark red stain I'd chosen for that night, now faded slightly from drinking. My lip print was on the rim of every glass, and I made a mental note to search for better-quality makeup. I perked my breasts up and adjusted the wide belt around my waist, then checked out my ass and thigh-high boots in the full-length mirror.

I'd fuck you, I could hear Lana saying earlier when she'd picked out the outfit.

"You look hot, girl," a woman, much drunker than me, said from the sinks.

I loved the camaraderie of drunken women in bathrooms.

"Thank you," I said as I adjusted my belt again. "So do you." I smiled at my new friend again, and the girl returned it before running back into the stall to vomit.

I grimaced at the sound and turned back to the mirror. With one last look, smoothing the seam of my leather skirt, I exited the bathroom.

Outside the bathroom, on the wall, was a neon red sign with hearts—the only light source in the darkened hall. I searched the more lit-up bar room as I walked toward it, wondering if Gavin had felt me reaching into his pocket. I hoped he had. I hoped he had read it and wanted to come find me.

A hand grabbed my arm. I was pulled backward, and my back slammed against the wall. Heart skipping, a toned body pressed flush to mine. The rich smell of Gavin's cologne piqued my senses as his shadow enveloped me, leaving only that red light to highlight the strongest parts of his features. His body molded to me in all the right places, meshing sinfully against mine.

Fuck, he smelled good.

My chest rose with my jagged breath, my thigh coming up and pressing between his. "Is this how you normally get women into your bed?" I breathed, chin craning upward to expose my neck. "Cornering them beneath the red lights… whispering dangerous quotes in their ears—" my back arched as I tried to press further into him, and I crawled one finger at a time up his shirt. "—*teasing* what you're capable of?"

I could see the hunger shadowed in his eyes, and the right corner of his lips flinched.

"Teasing? Is that why you put this in my pocket?" He closed his mouth, tongue working, and when he opened his mouth again, the pink candy heart that read 'TEASE ME' was gripped between his front teeth.

My lips threatened to lift as my gaze darted from his eyes to that heart. I debated whether to take it out of his mouth or remove myself from his grasp, make him watch me walk away as he had done to me.

I reached around his hips, intent on pulling him closer, but paused as I felt something in the opposite pocket from where I'd placed that heart earlier. Confusion slipped onto my face, and I pulled the object from within.

Fuzzy red handcuffs.

I bit my lips, brow elevating as I pulled the handcuffs out, and then I dangled them mockingly in his face. He popped the **TEASE ME** candy heart into his mouth, a soft chuckle sounding from the back of his throat.

My stomach knotted at the dangerous look in his eyes. The only image filling my mind right then was one of myself stretched out on the bed and feeling the soft fur on the cuffs around my wrists, his scruff on my inner thighs, those hands holding my ass as I squirmed against his tease and cried out his name…

"Something you're planning?" I asked.

He shifted his weight, head leaning closer. "*Every* fantasy," he promised. "You just have to be mine tonight."

I considered it, holding those cuffs as I slithered my hands up his chest. My high heel pressed into the wall with my bent leg. He wrapped his hands around my waist, squeezing the top of my ass as our hips pressed flushed together. That little squeeze and slight firmness against my abdomen were enough to make my mouth sag.

He was so close that with one move forward, I could have tasted him. His open mouth hovered in front of mine. I resisted giving in, knowing the moment our lips met that this game would be over.

I would be his.

I pushed on his chest, and Gavin stumbled off balance as he released me. That lopsided smirk dared to dance on his lips and in his eyes, and I turned on my heel to go back to the party.

But not before flicking another candy heart his way.

Chapter Seven
Gavin

BITE ME

This woman would be the death of me, I was sure of it.

I'd lived for centuries, delved in desires and toyed with mortals' emotions through all of them. But this woman… I needed her. I had to have her.

I decided I would use none of my godly tricks to get her. She would be mine of her own accord.

And damn, did I love the game we were playing.

She had stuck her tongue out and made a face at me as she'd flicked that candy heart my way, then turned, her hips swaying, making sure to step one long leg in front of the other—a deliberate tease I knew she was reveling in. Her sweater had even fallen a little more off her shoulder. And when she reached her friend, she took a long drink of water and pushed her hair to one side, exposing her neck—the neck I wanted to kiss and suck and choke.

I stayed by the bar so I could keep an eye on her from afar.

"Why are you still here?" Avril said as she approached him a little later. "What—I thought you'd left with that pretty girl already," she added. Her hand lifted to the bartender for another drink, and she leaned on the bar at my side.

I grinned, my gaze only briefly moving from Chloe to Avril. "Games," I said as I took a swig of my drink.

"I'm too old for games," she grunted, and I laughed softly. "Much rather be direct."

I leaned over the bar for a clean bag of the naughty candy hearts that we'd made as favors. "Games are fun, Av…" I said as I shoved the bag into my back pocket—

And I realized that fucking minx had kept the handcuffs.

I chuckled under my breath and shook my head at the floor.

"What's so funny?" Avril asked.

"She kept the fucking handcuffs," I said, my eyes landing on Chloe.

A quiet laugh escaped Avril, and she touched my arm as she made to walk away. "Don't let that one go."

It was twice within the next half hour that I moved across the room and brushed by her side, never stopping, but leaving a candy heart in her belt each time. And each time, she watched me with baited eyes, without saying a single word. She leaned into my touch with every pass, and I saw her chest heave when I approached—as though her body was responding to my simply being near.

The third time I started to go by her, she wasn't there, and I ended up circling the entire room before going back to the bar, my stomach knotting at the possibility that she had left.

Dammit. I'd fucked up by waiting too long to go to her. She'd slipped through my grasp—

I stopped in my tracks upon seeing her sitting in the chair by the bar that I'd been occupying just minutes prior. Her fingers were steepled beneath her chin as she watched me cross the rest of the way to her, a knowing smirk on those red pouting lips.

A flutter filled my stomach as I slowed my approach. She was too fucking cute. I couldn't wait to swipe that smug smile off her mouth as I filled it with my cock.

"You know, for a minute, I thought maybe you were scouting the floor for another woman to bother," she said as she toyed with the straw in her drink. "Then I realized you were looking for me."

I sat my glass on the bar and leaned against it slightly. "I believe you have something of mine."

"Took it for insurance."

"What for?"

"Making sure you didn't decide to leave without me."

My cock twitched at the hunger in her eyes.

She slowly uncrossed her legs and crossed them back, the edge of her skirt hiking just enough that I could see it was, in fact, stockings on her legs instead of tights. *Fuck me.* A lust-filled restriction sounded in the back of my throat at the sight of the clips attaching those stockings to whatever slutty lingerie she wore beneath those damn clothes.

I stepped closer. I needed her to know what she was doing to me, how those thighs were affecting my ability to think clearly, and how my dick was already stiffening with every fantasy flying through my head. I was caught in whatever web she'd spun around us, and I didn't dare try to break free.

"Sweet girl…" I dared to brush my knuckles on that exposed flesh… dared to flick my finger beneath the strap and give it a gentle tug. Her eyes held mine, and I said in a throaty rasp, "I don't plan on leaving here without you."

Her breath visibly caught as my hand moved higher. I never lost her stare. Her gaze blew wildly, lip tugging behind her teeth like she was thinking the same thing I was—if we could get away with my reaching fully beneath that skirt to see how wet she was.

I resisted, instead choosing to delicately caress her skin, savoring the softness beneath my fingers. But as I touched the bend of her hip, I reached into my back pocket.

"Put these in your bag with the handcuffs," I told her.

She eyed the red drawstring baggie, and when she opened it, delight lifted on every inch of her face.

"What are these for?" she asked.

I felt my lips tug upwards, and I leaned closer, turning so that both of my hands were on her thighs. "I plan on doing everything that these hearts say. Striping you. Biting you. Sucking you. All of them… One at a time… One command after the other… Over and over until you beg me to stop," I said in her ear. "And when you do, I'll—"

"Let me guess," she interjected. "You'll make me see God?"

"Baby, tonight, I am your god," I said, squeezing her flesh. "And you're the woman who's going to bring Eros to his knees."

Her tongue darted over her lips, and I refrained from capturing it with my teeth. "I like the sound of that," she said.

"I thought you might."

Her neck extended in my direction, our noses nearly brushing, but I didn't let her get any closer. A heavy sigh left me as I forced myself to straighten over her, still stroking her thighs. I couldn't stop touching her— didn't want to stop touching her. At this point, I feared letting her go might mean her disappearing from in front of me.

"I just need one thing from you," I said.

"What's that?"

"Say you're mine."

I was ready to beg for her. Plead on my knees for her. I didn't know how much more of this dance I could take.

I wanted to touch her everywhere. Taste her in every way. Soak her up as she spilled on my tongue and cried out my name. I needed to feel her body around me. Just the warmth of her flesh had me on edge. It was taking everything not to press further, to uncross her legs so I could stand between them or whisper my hand across the nipples I knew were hardened beneath her fucking bra.

Chloe's smile widened. She shifted, and as her feet hit the ground, I wrapped my arm around her waist. I wanted her answer. I wanted *her*. Her breasts brushed against my chest, and I squeezed her waist as she tickled her fingers over my forearm, my hair rising with her every touch.

Every time I looked at her, she became more and more beautiful—so beautiful, I was sure that had my mother known about her, she'd have become jealous, perhaps even tried to destroy her beauty with some poison or devastating disease.

"Cherry vodka," the bartender announced as she set a drink in front of us and left with two slaps to the bar top.

Our gaze broke, and Chloe reached for the glass, but I couldn't look away. And when she picked up the juicy cherry from inside her drink, my insides lit on fire. She pressed the dripping red fruit to her puckered lips, letting it sit for a moment before sucking it back and crushing it in her teeth.

Red liquid dribbled from the corner of her mouth. My knees weakened, and I nearly fell to the floor before her. I had to contain my urge to lick the sweetness off her face.

She caught the drip with her tongue, her lashes lifting and hitting her eyelids when she smiled at me.

Gods, that fucking smile.

That fucking… *her.*

She knew she was making me crazy, and shit… I loved it.

"Thanks for the drink," was all she said before hugging that glass to her chest and pushing past me, back to the table with Lana.

I scoffed aloud, my head sinking to my chest as amusement spread through me from her cheekiness. I was going to have her ass pink later for the torture she was putting me through. Gods, I couldn't wait to hear that moan.

"Bad luck tonight?" the bartender asked as she dried off a glass.

I stared out at Chloe again. "I think she's testing to see how long it'll take me to break," I said.

The bartender grinned. "How's that going for you?"

"I'm fucking shattered," I admitted.

The bartender laughed, her short blue curls bouncing when she threw her head back. "It's Valentine's Day,

Cupid," she jested. "Shouldn't the god of desire himself get the girl?"

A joke to my job title, I knew, but the salutation filled me with pride, nonetheless. I glanced back at Chloe one more time, then asked the bartender to put both our tabs on mine before I made my final descent into Chloe's magnetic abyss.

Lana was laughing at a joke when I approached their table a few minutes later. I snuck in behind Chloe while she was distracted and wrapped my hands around her waist, squeezing her soft flesh. Without looking, she seemed to know who it was and leaned back into me, her hand grazing over mine.

"Hello, Cupid," she said as I bent down to her ear.

"You know… all this begging you're making me do…" I said into her hair, "I might have to punish you for it later. You've been a *very* bad girl, teasing me all night."

Her head moved sideways just so, and I could see a smile lift at the corner of her lips. "Tell me how you'll punish me," she said in a voice only I could hear.

"Over my knees," I said, clutching her waist. "And you'll only be wearing those fluffy handcuffs."

Her ass shifted back into me, making my cock twitch at the pressure.

"Promise?" she asked.

I held her hip firm as I pressed into her, and I chuckled under my breath before replying, "Sweet girl… I *swear* it."

A soft laugh escaped her. She turned to her right, reaching into the candy dish on the bar top. She chose a heart, and as she circled into me, she placed it on her tongue.

I'M YOURS

Every muscle in my body snapped to attention. I held my composure and watched her a quiet second before reaching into the bowl myself to look for a particular heart—a heart that I intended to keep plenty of on hand for the rest of the night.

When I found it, I held her gaze and placed the candy on my tongue.

GOOD GIRL

She looked like the heart had triggered her to the very depths of her soul. Her chest visibly caved with her exhale, brown eyes dancing from my eyes to my lips. And just as I started to curl the candy back into my mouth, she grabbed my sweater, pulled me down, and her open mouth crashed into mine.

Chapter Eight
Chloe

I didn't know what had come over me—why seeing that particular heart on his tongue had sent my entire body into overdrive.

But it did.

Fuck, it did.

His hands wrapped around my waist, my neck. He was clutching my flesh, his tongue sweeping against mine, fingers tugging gently at the roots of my hair. Those lips… those *hands*… I could hardly wait to have them trailing every inch of me. My cunt throbbed with every glide of his tongue against mine, the taste of the candy and vodka on his tongue. A sick adrenaline shivered over me, making me forget that we were in the middle of a crowded bar. Until he slowed his eagerness, and he finally pulled back.

Cold air swept between us, and my body instantly craved his attachment again. Our breaths were short, exasperated. His forehead rested against mine; his digits still clamped on my hips. I was practically on fire from that kiss. Shit, that kiss had me spinning.

I needed more.

My clenched fists tightened on his sweater again. I leaned up and licked his open mouth, making him move in again to kiss me, but I swayed back.

"My place."

Lana barely did more than give me a kiss on the cheek and tell me to be safe—reminding me to use protection, which I was definitely up to date on—as Gavin disappeared to get his coat from the seat he'd occupied before.

I shot back the last swig of my drink, making a face at the sting of the last drops on my tongue. I had no sooner thrown my coat over my arm before a hand grabbed me by the elbow and whirled me around. Gavin hauled me flush, his lips pressing against mine in a claiming kiss that limped my knees.

That dangerous, crooked smirk flashed down at me when he released my lips. I barely had a moment to consider jumping his bones again before he leaned down and whispered in my ear.

"Walk us to my Jeep. Give me a preview of that ass swaying like it'll do on my lap later."

I forgot how damn cold it was outside.

The chilled air hit my cheeks as soon as we exited the packed bar. Sounds muted in the absence of music and laughter, replaced with the noise of cars passing by. I tugged on Gavin's hand and looked back at him, noticing how he was watching my every move, that dilation filling his eyes like he could consume my soul if he tried. My heart throbbed in my ears every time he squeezed my fingers. I had to stop myself from nearly skipping to the black Jeep Wrangler parked beneath a streetlamp.

The Jeep's lights flickered when he unlocked the doors, and with one glance over my shoulder at his darkened eyes, I let his hand go and reached for the handle. It opened—

Gavin crashed into my back. The door snapped close as he trapped me between his heated body and the cold metal. A groan escaped me at the strength of him over me, his nose in my hair, hands on my hips, and fisting my skirt in his grasp. I arched back into him, my mouth agape when his lips pressed to my neck. I ground my ass against his pelvis just as he raised my skirt a fraction —only enough that the bare part of my thighs above my stockings was exposed. A shiver washed over me with the wind blowing, but it didn't pull me from the moment. I reached back and snaked my arm up, hand resting behind his head and grabbing his hair as my body rocked against his. The fact that we were on the street in front of everyone did little to deter me from nearly bending over and letting him fuck me against his car. I could feel his length stiffening between my ass cheeks, his size making a whimper leave me.

"Do you want it right here," he asked in a breath. His touch traveled from my hips to my front, one finger whispering over the tiny lace thong I was wearing. I flinched at the tickle of his hands, ready to plead for him to continue.

"Should I bend you over the front of my car?" he whispered. "Would you like everyone to watch?"

"Yes," she answered.

His finger dipped beneath the lace, making my eyes roll. Oh, *fuck*. A restlessness sank into my knees. I groaned again, and he chuckled into my neck as the pad of his thumb grazed my throbbing clit. Fucking hell, I needed him.

"Shit, Chloe," he groaned. "You're so wet for me. I could slide inside you so easily… Hold my hand over your mouth… Tease you until tears fall down your beautiful cheeks, and you beg for more…" His rasp shivered over my body, and my hips moved involuntarily against his touch.

"Will you beg for me tonight, baby?"

The window fogged from my heated breath as my body melted into his embrace. He flipped me around, making me jolt into the car door with the strength of his hands. I was pinned beneath him, my wrists restrained by my head. He kissed me again, biting and eager. His stiffness pressed into my abdomen, making my leg bend up around his waist so he could push further into me. The wind had no chance at separating us as he released my left wrist and wrapped that hand beneath my thigh, hiking it higher around his waist. And when he let go of my other wrist, allowing me to hold his face instead, he squeezed my ass so hard that I moaned into his mouth.

I had just pulled back when I felt his touch on my jaw, his thumb stroking my bottom lip.

"Once you get in this car… you're all mine."

My fingers breezed his stomach before diving beneath his shirt. The warmth of his skin met my chilled fingers, and his abs flinched at my touch. I tilted my head back to look at him, nails scratching his skin, and I wrapped my lips around his thumb.

His chest collapsed heavily as I sucked his finger, and I whispered, "Show me your shadow in the dark… *Eros.*"

I thought his gaze had held licentious desire and wickedness in them before… but at the very mention of what he said was his true name, all green evacuated beneath his widened pupils, and he laughed.

The man *laughed*.

It was a laugh that cradled my bones in a sudden craving for every part of him. A laugh that heated and curled my blood, quickened my heart, and called to the deepest parts of my soul. I had wanted him before… but now…

Now, I would do everything to have him.

"Oh, sweet girl—"

His hand slid down my neck and tightened on my throat, making my breath hitch, my heart stumble, and as he hovered over me, that dimple shone beneath his scruff.

"—You're going to regret calling me that."

Fuck, he was hot.

The kiss he pressed to my lips was fleeting, and he held my face in his hand as he said, "Put your address in," before opening the door for me. He was still watching me as I crawled in, a seriousness taking over his eyes, his mouth sagging with every labored breath. He pinched my ass, making me yelp, then gave me a wink and closed the door.

The click of that door sent a pulse through me. Adrenaline and desire mingled and entwined through my veins like they were carrying poison straight to my staggering heart. I was nearly giddy with want for this man.

I sat up on my knees in the seat and started punching in my address on the GPS screen once he'd entered the driver's seat and turned over the engine. Rock music blared in the speakers, and neither of us bothered turning it down. His seatbelt clicked. He put the car in drive, and as he pulled out into traffic, a sharp ache of excitement surged through me. My body threw back into the seat at his acceleration. I laughed unexpectedly, and Gavin just smirked at me in response.

The bass vibrated the entire car. He swerved through downtown. Every flashing red light and headlight passing by and reflecting off his features had my eager body restless. They highlighted every beautiful line on his face, making me crave him even more. I pushed back up to my knees and leaned over in his direction, wanting to tease him as he'd been teasing me. He opened up to me without hesitation, and as he wrapped his right hand around my waist, I bent over the console.

His skin tasted like he smelled—like candy and musk and dangerous peppered vanilla spice. He tasted like dessert, and I wanted to know if he tasted like that everywhere. I reached into his pants, a moan escaping me when I felt his cock erecting beneath my hand.

And when we slowed to a stoplight, he took both his hands off the steering wheel and wrapped them around my face, kissing me. Desperately. Like this was his last night on earth. I sucked his tongue as I pulled away, and our eyes met beneath a sliver of the red glare from the light.

"Slide back," I whispered before kissing him again.

He groaned into my mouth, but I felt the seat jerk as he shifted.

A horn blew.

All anxiety evacuated my body as I looked up for the soft-top controls. I hit the button, rolling the roof back just enough to get my hand through, and I flipped off the person behind us just as Gavin jammed on the accelerator. I was thrown back into the seat again, laughing and hanging onto his arm to keep myself steady.

"So, Cupid..." I smiled slyly and shifted back up to his side. I kissed his scruff-covered cheek, unbuttoning his pants as he slipped his right arm back around my waist. I pressed my palm to his length, groaning at the feeling of his size and length. I loved the way he responded to me, so much so that teasing him through his underwear wasn't enough. I pulled his cock from the slit in his boxer briefs. My hand wrapped firmly around his tip, and he moaned in my ear.

"You like that?" I whispered as I turned to watch his eyes flutter. His answer came in another groan as I continued to stroke him. I relished that power over him, knowing one slip of the wheel could have sent us crashing into another vehicle.

I craved that thrill—being exposed and teetering on the edge of oblivion. It was a thrill that I hadn't felt in a long time. He made me feel invincible and sexy, desired and powerful. It was hot, and I was soaking from the intensity of him.

I settled on my knees, arched my back, and lifted my ass high in the air as I bent down to his lap. And when my lips enclosed around his tip, he cursed my name.

"Oh, fuck yes… Chloe," he whispered as he fisted the bottom of my skirt, exposing my thong and the straps over my bare ass that attached to my stockings. He massaged my ass and then smacked it hard, making me moan around his dick.

"Just like that," he uttered as he smacked my ass again. "Gods, *yes.*"

The force of his spank had me soaking more than I already was. I lowered my mouth, stretching over his girth, slowly tonguing his taut cock. I wiggled my backside as he toyed with the thong between my cheeks.

His dick hit the back of my throat. Again and again. And the further I took him into oblivion, the further he reached over around my ass. He curled those fingers and grazed my entrances, cursing when he felt my wetness. Just as he seemed to think about teasing me, I took him all the way in again, gagging on his thickness taking up and swelling down my throat, and his hand moved from my ass to the back of my head.

"Fuck, baby." His voice was hardly more audible than a whisper as his hips moved in my direction. His fingers wrapped in my hair, his legs spreading wide to adjust himself.

"You want my cock deeper, sweet girl?" he asked as the car slowed for another stoplight.

I pulled back slowly, head tilting as I tongued his tip. "Yes," I answered.

"You like showing off that pussy in the dark, don't you?" he asked. "Does it make you wetter? Knowing how many people are salivating at that ass in the window? At how many people have been staring and watching you suck my dick at these stoplights?"

I groaned around his cock again at the thought as I started sucking on him once more. Thankfully, the window was at least a little tinted, so my ass wasn't completely out. However, I couldn't deny that I liked the idea that people could see my silhouette like this. I'd never really been a public play person, but this… this was intoxicating. I could have done this all night—fucked him with the roof totally off, not just the soft-top rolled back. I wanted to watch people get off at the sight of me riding him, put on a show for the rest of this fucking town.

The fantasy of fucking him like that made me hum on his length and take him deeper. Knowing how the stop lights and streetlamps would cascade on us and reflect off the drops of water and puddles left behind by the snow… How that cold, misty air would tease my skin… how his fingers would dig into my ass—

His middle finger dipped inside me, and he chuckled deeply, his cock twitching in my mouth. "Gods, that *is* making you wetter. Do you think you deserve to choke on my cock for that?"

My answer hummed around his length, and I felt the seat move as his head hit the headrest, hand tightening in my hair again. The grip sent a shiver over my skin. The slow help and guidance of his grasp begged me to take him deeper, to salivate around his dick and choke when he held me there too long.

And I fucking did.

I let him push me. I let him choke me. I let him hold me there until saliva dribbled out of my mouth, until my eyes teared up, and I had to grip his leg to come up for air. I gasped for breath upon coming up and felt the rumble of his chuckle beside me.

"You're such a good, *sweet* girl..." he cooed, and I didn't understand how those words sent my pulse into overdrive.

As he made a slow turn onto the highway, he grasped my chin and turned me to look at him. His thumb wiped away the tear that had escaped when I hadn't been able to breathe.

"Make me come, baby," he whispered. "Make me forget I'm driving this car. Send us both into oblivion."

A fleeting kiss was pressed to my lips before I lowered myself again. He tugged on my hair as I worked him, causing a tingle to rise on my skin and my pussy to throb. Every inch of him, I sucked and swirled my tongue. Though, this time, I wasn't teasing. I wasn't savoring. I meant to bring him to his end—to send him crashing to that end. Crashing and writhing and begging me to stop as he spilled. I wanted his legs shaking and his knuckles white against the steering wheel. Wanted him gripping my hair until I cried out in pain.

"Shit, baby "

The car was speeding up as he tried to deny his end. It only made me more eager. I had him right at his edge. I could feel him straining, his hips bucking erratically.

"Oh, fuck, like that," he was suddenly saying. "Holy gods, Chloe—Like that—*fuck*—"

The engine was at a roar. We were swerving, speeding, and every second had me taking him further toward that abyss. His head threw back into the headrest as an urgency took over. He cursed my name again, his hand slamming into the steering wheel, his cock taut.

I had him—*had* him—

He spilled with a loud groan and slapped my ass so hard that I felt it quake in my bones. But I didn't stop. He was trembling, moaning my name like it was his saving grace. The car was slowing as I devoured his cum, swallowing and continuing to suck until I had taken every last drop.

"Shit—*Chloe*—"

The car stopped. Both his hands pulled me up by the hair, and I couldn't stop my devious laughter from sounding as I sat back on my knees in the passenger seat and admired the absolute satiated bewilderment on his beautiful face.

Chapter Nine

Gavin

Holy fuck.

I'd had to pull over.

I hadn't come that hard in years, and she'd swallowed it like it was nourishment.

We were parked on the side of the highway, hazards blinking.

And she was grinning as if she'd just won the fucking lottery.

A dribble of my cum seeped from the corner of her sinful mouth. Her scarlet-stained lips were smeared, and there was a gentle spray of her mascara beneath her glistening, yet delighted, eyes.

I fought to catch my breath and clear the stars in my eyes as I put the Jeep in park, and I nearly ripped the seatbelt out of its lock to get to her. She was magnetic... poison... a drug I would be consuming like water the rest of the night. Her mouth was ecstasy itself. The memory alone of everything she'd just done with her tongue had me twitching and aching for her again.

I leaned over and kissed her hard, groaning when she pushed her hands into my hair. Her short nails scratched my skin, and the sensation drove me crazy. I was out of my seat in less than a second. Hovering over her, pushing her back, grabbing her hips and pulling her legs into the air. I needed to feel how wet she was from that, because I had a feeling she was drenched.

Gods, I loved being right.

She was fucking soaking through those panties. I continued to kiss her as I delved a finger inside her heat, my thumb pressing against that swollen clit. I kissed down her jaw to her neck, sucking on her skin and tasting the sweat in the dip of her collarbone. I was ready to lick every part of her, ready to consume her until she had nothing left. And I would... fucking gods, I would. I would have her wholly undone and begging me to stop—

"Gavin..." She arched her back into me with the moan of my name, tugging at the roots of my hair, and when I looked up at her again, intent on kissing her, I had to pause.

There was a candy heart on her outstretched tongue.

TASTE ME

My head sank between her full breasts. I groaned against her skin, inhaling the scent of her, savoring the feel of those pillows around my cheeks. I tore myself away before there was no turning back and glanced up at the GPS.

Five miles.

I leaned up and kissed her again. "I will, baby," I promised before settling back in my seat. "Put on your seatbelt," I said, to which she narrowed her eyes. "Seatbelt," I repeated. "Five miles of road lie between me having you. If you think I'm driving slow the rest of the way, you're wrong. Put on your seatbelt."

She didn't argue, and as the belt locked in place, I couldn't help from smirking over at her and whispering, "That's my girl," as I put the car in drive and jolted out onto the highway.

The thrust of the car threw her back into the seat again. That fucking laugh escaped her mouth, and I reached over to her thigh as we sped off.

The noise of the engine humming at its limit mixed with the roar of the blaring music fueled my desperation. It may have only been a few miles, but it felt like a lifetime.

Time slowed to a near standstill when she spread her legs and moved my hand higher.

"Don't stop," she said in a begging moan that chilled my skin.

Blood rushed to my cock again as I dipped my finger beneath the fabric. Her head arched back into the seat, and she grabbed her knees.

"Guide me, baby," I said, pulling her hand between her legs and atop mine. "Show me what you like." Her wetness surrounded my finger as she moved it. Stroking down, dipping into her entrance, then back up to her hardened clit.

"You like it right there?" I asked, and her hips moved against my hand. I scoffed under my breath at her closed eyes and grinding hips. "You're so wet for me, baby," I said as I made a turn into her complex lot. "Tell me which building is yours."

"Make a right—fuck, *there*," she breathed, and I wasn't sure if she meant my hand or the building. "Go around this corner—Building 3818—"

I squeezed her clit between my fingers, leading her hand to clench around my wrist and holding me in place.

"You're so greedy," I said as I swerved into a parking place.

I couldn't get upstairs fast enough.

She was out of the car before me, shuffling her skirt down and throwing her bag onto her shoulder. Everything was a haze as I followed her into her elevator. I barely even saw the other cars or noticed the apartments.

There was only her. Only this.

The elevator dinged, and I grabbed her by the neck and pulled her around and into me, unable to resist kissing her. Her hands on my hips, my palms on her cheeks… We backed into the cage, and she broke free just long enough to press the button to her floor, but I stayed on her, tasting her neck where some of her drink had spilled onto her skin, my fingers once more lifting up that damn skirt.

"How many floors do we have?" I asked her.

"Ten," she breathed as she hiked her leg around my waist.

The doors closed, and I pulled back to smirk down at her as I noticed the camera over the door. "Don't come, sweet girl."

"What—Fuck, *Gavin*—"

Her chin craned upwards the moment I pressed two fingers inside her. Shit, she was wet. I had to remind myself not to take her all at once. I bit her throat and pulsed that finger in and out, my thumb on her clit. Her moan sent me cursing. She bucked into my hand, and I could feel her walls throbbing.

"You like this, don't you? You like being watched?" I said upon hearing her whimper at denying herself. "Do you think the security guard is enjoying the show?"

Chloe pushed on my shoulder. "Shit—what—" But her body limped when I curled my fingers deeper inside her again. "Gavin—"

"Tell me you want me to stop," I said against her neck. "Tell me you don't want to be watched. Tell me you're not throbbing at the thrill of knowing someone is probably getting off to the sound of your beautiful fucking moans and the sight of your open mouth." I pulled back, meeting her eyes, and she sucked her lip behind her teeth as she tried to suppress a moan.

"Don't stop," she said in a breathless high-pitch.

I chuckled softly at her plea and slowed my caress. "Go ahead, baby," I whispered. "Scream for me." I pinched her clit again, making her jaw shake and her mouth sag. "Give your audience what they want."

The elevator dinged, and Chloe flinched, nearly jumping out of my arms, but I smiled against her skin and pulled my hand from beneath her skirt. She whimpered, her eyes opening, and I held that gaze as I brought my fingers to my lips to taste.

"Mmm…" I sang at the taste of what I'd done to her. "Like candy."

Chloe's lips slammed into mine once more as she grabbed me by the sweater and pushed me backward into the hall. We were out of the elevator, slamming into the opposite wall. A picture fell. A vase on the buffet table broke. The wall vibrated. She was clawing and tugging at my neck and hair. Lips smashing together with such recklessness that I had to refrain from bending her over that table and fucking her in the hall.

Before I could, she moved from beneath me and took my hand.

One turn. Two turns. The red-walled halls reminded me of the neon at the bar, only adding to my desire for this woman. She was heading toward the door at the end of the dead, darkened hall, and upon reaching it, she dropped my hand to search for her keys.

I hovered over her, my forearm lying against the doorframe, the other gripping at her hip. I couldn't wait to have her undressed and restrained on the bed, to feel her skin flush to mine, hear her moan without holding back…

The fantasies filled my head, distracting me from her fumbling figure—so much so that when she got the door unlocked, I had to snap myself out of the daze.

The smell of spiced vanilla air freshener hit me as the door opened. I nearly fell when she turned and grabbed me by the shirt, yanking me inside. The door slammed, and she pushed me onto the back of it, her lips meeting mine.

Whatever papers she'd had pinned to the fridge fell to the ground. Her hair tangled in my fingers as I pulled her closer. Hands sliding down her side, I grabbed her ass and hauled her up onto my waist. Her breasts pushed into my face, and I buried my head between them, biting the top of her tit where I could see stretch marks on her skin. The sight of them made me clench her ass tighter. Fucking gods, she made me wild. I groaned at the thought of licking every mark on her body, tasting every inch of her delicate flesh, and savoring that swollen cunt. My cock was already pressing against my zipper at the thought.

I lifted my head from her breasts, intent on kissing her again, but she pushed her hands to my face and held me steady.

"I need five minutes," she managed, her heavy breaths jagged between us.

I swallowed, my chest heaving, and I nodded as I set her on the ground again. A break. A break could be good. I could take a moment and collect myself, look at the bedroom and get my bearings.

"Five," I agreed.

But before she could walk away from me, I hauled her back into my arms, my fingers pulling in her hair and exposing her neck.

"If you even think about touching yourself in there, I'll punish you the rest of the night," I warned. "And not the kind of punishment you think you'll enjoy."

I relaxed his grip and slid my hand against her cheek, thumb brushing her lip, and she opened her mouth to suck on my finger. A restriction sounded in the back of my throat as I recalled how she'd sucked on that cherry, how her lips had felt around my cock…

"Five minutes," she repeated. "Get the candy out of my bag."

I smiled and leaned down, acting like I would kiss her again, but I paused as our lips brushed.

"Three."

Chapter Ten
Chloe

I nearly fell to the ground trying to get my boots off once I was in the bathroom.

The cold floor was perfect on my flat feet. I sank my back against the door, closing my eyes to take a moment to get myself together. I could still taste his cum on my tongue, and still feel his lips like a brand on my neck.

I let the room spin as I came down from the high that had been the entire hazy evening.

Thank fuck I'd been drinking water between those cocktails. Even the bar felt so far away, like it had been hours since we'd left. The memory of his hand between my legs filled my mind, his slaps on my ass as I'd taken him deep. I wanted to do that again. I wanted to feel his dick down my throat again, but this time I wanted to watch his face as I brought him crashing down. I needed to see him throw his head back and close his eyes, all so I could tell him to open his eyes and watch me take him deep.

I slipped my hand between my thighs just to see if I was as wet as I thought I was. Only even as I started to touch myself, a thought hit me.

He was wandering around my apartment. Alone.

Shit, when was the last time I'd cleaned the fucking wine stains off the carpet?

Being a workaholic, I rarely had guests over, and sometimes things simply got out of hand. Thankfully, I'd at least taken time to tidy up and clean the clothes off the floor a couple of days before.

Breathe, I reminded myself.

I pushed off the door and started shoving the dirty towels from the floor into the bin, then straightened up the sink. I took a swig of Listerine and let it swish in my mouth as I moved things around. And after I spat, I stared at myself in the mirror.

Dammit, I was a mess. A hot fucking mess. My lip stain was smeared, some of my mascara had smudged beneath my eyes. My hair was flat.

Three minutes.

I was well past that.

Music thudded the walls. He must have found my speakers and connected his phone to them. I almost laughed as I imagined whatever he was doing out there on his own.

Good thing the neighbors were away.

I sprayed some dry shampoo in my hair and cleaned off my smeared lips. Heat beat on my cheeks as the warmth of the apartment finally hit me, and I stripped out of my sweater and skirt, leaving only the red and black lingerie on my body.

I loved this set. The thigh-high stockings and attached strappy belt that stretched over my abdomen to just above my belly button, sheer black thong and a red and black push-up corset bra.

One last flip of my hair, one more look in the mirror, and I exited the bathroom.

Gavin wasn't on the bed when I opened the door. I squinted into the darkness, noticing he'd placed some of the candy hearts on the bed and turned on one of her bedside lamps. The music blared—music that had me feeling more aroused than I had before.

Perhaps he was Cupid.

I found him in the kitchen reading over the ingredients on a drink from the fridge, and I paused to admire him for a minute.

He'd taken his sweater off, showcasing the tattoos on his arms that looked like geometric suns, moons, roses, bow and arrows, wings… like figure drawings from Roman times, dissected and in segments. Soft tufts of ginger hair lightly sprayed his toned chest. I could even see a splattering of freckles on his shoulders.

Those fucking shoulders.

His hips were pushed forward, and I bit my bottom lip as I leaned on the doorframe and took in the rest of him.

Gavin glanced twice in my direction, apparently having seen me move in the corner of his eyes. The stare he held me with caused me to shift and rub my thighs together, desperate for any friction. His tongue darted out over his lips, and he sat the drink on the counter.

"That was longer than three minutes," he said, and my lips twisted smugly in response.

"What are you going to do about it?" I dared.

Gavin shifted, his head tilting as he looked me wholly over, eyes lingering on my breasts, then my hips, and I watched as a pleased look rose over his features.

I wanted to slap it off his stupidly beautiful face.

"Come here," he said with a gesture of his fingers, and the way he said it made my stomach knot.

I prowled toward him, cursing my fluttering heart the entire way. Upon reaching him, he slid one hand around my waist, grabbing my ass while the other tickled up my side… from my waist to my ribs, to my breast that he cupped in his hand before continuing up to my neck. He lingered there and tilted my chin back as I grabbed onto his belt.

That damn dimple appeared with a lift of his lips.

"Exactly how fucking tall were those heels?"

My mouth dropped, and I shoved his chest as he laughed. "You're such an ass," I laughed. "I'm not short!" But he grabbed me fast, his strong arms lifting me beneath my backside. I was wrapped around his waist again before I had a chance to get away, and his lips captured mine.

My ass hit the counter. He leaned over, his hands pressing on either side of me—our kisses long and deep, unlike before when they had been a whirlwind of teeth and tongues. Just as I thought he might let that hand trail between my legs, he pulled back and dangled a small red satchel in front of me.

"Pick three," he said, his voice a vibration on my skin.

Excitement pulsed through me and settled as warmth pooled between my legs, a knot of that thrill weaving in my chest. I reached inside the bag for the naughty candy heart, and then sat them one at a time on the counter.

LICK ME

Fuck yes.

TEASE ME

Even he groaned at that one.

TASTE ME

I frowned at the last candy. "That's the same as the first," I argued, tossing it back in the bag. "I'm trying again."

"Knew you were a cheater," he said as he squeezed my thighs.

My heart dropped at the one I pulled out next.

BEG FOR IT

A devious chuckle left Gavin's lips... throaty and dangerous... and my heart constricted when I looked up at him. All green had evacuated his pupils, replaced with an abyss of pure lust that made my breath catch.

"Maybe I'll put that one back—"

He grabbed my wrist as I made to change the heart out, and even though I knew we were teasing, the look in his eyes caused me to shift. He reached behind him and pulled something from his pocket—

The handcuffs.

The red fur was soft against my skin when he latched the cuffs on my wrist. I swallowed as anticipation swelled within me. This was actually happening. I tried not to overthink it and stay in the moment. And with the way he was looking at me, it really wasn't hard.

"Repeat after me, baby," he said softly. "Arrow."

I frowned but repeated the word anyway. "Arrow… what's that?"

"Your safe word," he explained. "Use it any time you're uncomfortable, and I will stop. No questions asked."

My heart stumbled. There was a seriousness in his gaze that made me realize he was completely serious, and for some reason, I trusted that.

"Okay," I said.

Gavin leaned in and gave me a soft kiss as he locked my other hand in the cuff. Secured and wholly his. He stood back and started rubbing my thighs up and down, that smirk lifting his lips once more.

"So, *Chloe*… Are you ready to play?"

Chapter Eleven

Gavin

"Yes."

I stifled a groan at the word, at the whispered way she said it, and I leaned in to kiss her fiercely before hauling her into my arms and then throwing her over my shoulder. A high-pitched squeal escaped her, along with my name, and I smacked her ass with such force that she flinched. A greedy moan came from her mouth in response to the sting, making blood rush to my cock as I imagined what even more might do to her.

I tickled my hand across her reddening cheek, squeezing that soft flesh, and then I spanked her again upon crossing into the bedroom. I threw her on the bed with a bounce, noting that smile on her face beneath her silky black hair. As I let her go and stood back, I took in the sight of her in that lingerie again.

That *fucking* lingerie.

Gods, I'd nearly forgotten myself right then. Had nearly thrown all intentions of teasing her out of the window. The way the black straps on her stomach and hips creased in her skin, how her cleavage heaved behind that bra, the stockings—fucking Styx, the *stockings*—they wrapped her thighs like beacons telling me where to taste her first.

I needed to bite down on something and scream out my frustrations just to keep myself from breaking down and taking her like some sort of untamed animal.

I had to slow down.

She rolled her head, her hair sprawling around her, and I sat on the edge of the bed. She gazed up at me, clearly confused, and I patted my thigh without a word, beckoning her to sit on it.

Chloe looked like she might argue as she sat up on her knees. "What—are you actually going to spank me?"

"Come here."

Her brows knitted, but she shuffled hesitantly in my direction. There was a delight in her gaze when she paused at my side. I wondered if she knew she shouldn't be enjoying this, and she was anyway.

What a fucking treat.

"Did I do something wrong?" she asked innocently.

I grabbed her by the throat and yanked the handcuffs, pulling her forward so that she was merely a breath from my face. She gasped, and I loosened my grip on her neck to wrap up around her jaw instead, feeling my smile lift at her pupils, seeming to blow with both surprise and desire.

"You thought I was joking earlier…"

Chloe swallowed, tongue darting out over those plump red lips. "Yes," came her breathy response.

I resisted sucking her tongue between my own lips or biting that gorgeous pout. "Did you think you could be such a bad girl and get away with it?" I asked.

Her breaths were getting heavier, that delight waning just slightly from her eyes and turning into a deep lust, an almost fearful lust, but she didn't respond. My chuckle sounded more sadistic than I'd planned as my fingers tightened on her face.

"Answer me, baby," I said.

"Yes," she said eagerly.

My grip relaxed on her cheeks, and I scoffed softly. "Gods, you're even fucking cute when you're scared," I said.

As my eyes traveled over her, I noted the squeeze of her thighs, the tremble of her arms, and the almost purse of her dry lips, and I wondered how much wetter she was just from that. I released her face, stroked her reddened skin, and gave her a fleeting kiss that she leaned forward for again as though she wanted more.

"Over my knees like a good girl."

She held my gaze as she stretched her arms in front of her, rising on her knees, and then she sank her outstretched arms over my lap to the mattress. Her ass wiggled in the air, making me stifle my own stiffening cock at her bent over and waiting.

I wanted to take a picture of how fucking perfect this was.

I dragged my fingers through her hair, my other hand grazing teasingly across her ass. My wrist flicked with the first slap, and Chloe jumped.

"Did you enjoy teasing me all night?" I asked.

Another.

But Chloe… Chloe didn't seem to care. Didn't seem to mind the sting or tingle on her skin.

"Yes," she groaned out, and the little moan that escaped her with it was music to my ears. She sounded like she was trying to hide how much she was enjoying herself.

"Did you take your time in that bathroom to test me?"

Another—*harder*.

"*Fuck*—" an undeniable moan sounded this time, but she said, "No," quickly before I could comment.

Her ass was reddening so. *Fucking. Beautifully*.

"Did you touch yourself in there?" I spanked her again, and she flinched at the sternness of my hand.

"I—no," she answered.

Maybe that was enough for the moment. The way her body responded… My dick ached at the sight. I ran my finger between her tingling cheeks. "Let's see how swollen that pretty cunt is…"

Gods, she was soaking.

I cursed as I dipped my finger inside her, and then swirled that wetness on her clit. "You're fucking drenching," I muttered. "Are you always this wet, baby?"

"Gavin—"

I tugged her up slowly, my hand still delicately touching her tingling ass, and I moved her legs to where she was straddled over my lap, pushing her handcuffed arms around my neck. Some of her mascara had smattered beneath her eyes again, and I reached up to smudge it with my thumb.

"That was only a taste," I whispered. "The next time you're over my knees, it won't be for pleasure. Tell me you understand."

Chloe's throat moved with her swallow. "Yes," she uttered.

I leaned forward and kissed her softly before whispering, "Good girl," against her lips.

Her eyes fluttered like they'd done at the bar when I'd held that candy heart on my tongue. She grabbed the back of my head and pulled me to her again, her needing lips crashing against mine. I shifted her flush and touched her pussy again.

"You're going to come so hard for me, baby," I said as I teased her nerves. She bit her lip, rocking against my hand, and nodded vigorously.

"Yes," she gasped.

"I bet your beg sounds as delightful as that smart mouth."

Her shoulders fell as though she had just remembered our game, and her hands scratched in my hair, tongue licking her lips as she took a second to collect herself. She began to nod slowly, her breath intake sharp, as she whispered a quick, "Yes," before kissing me again.

Her desperation was a thrill. The way she wanted it—wanted *me*—was something I hadn't experienced in so long.

I lifted her around my waist as I stood, and she held tight, continuing our kiss and allowing me full control over her. Those handcuffs brushed the back of my neck, and I knelt on the bed with her. Her back hit the mattress before I moved from beneath her jointed wrists.

Her eyes never left me as I pressed my hands into the bed by her breasts, and I hovered so close to her face that she leaned up to kiss me again, but I moved before she could.

"Grab those bars, baby. Over your head," I said with a nod to her black-railed headboard.

Once her fingers latched around one of the black bars, I smirked at her, saying, "Just like that. Don't let go."

She arched her back, and I chuckled at her eagerness. "You're fucking greedy for me," I teased as I pulled the key to the handcuffs from my front pocket. I unhooked one cuff to link it behind the bar, and when she was secure, I took a moment to enjoy the view in front of me.

"You look so sexy like this," I said upon settling back on my knees between her bent thighs, my hands traveling up her legs. "Splayed out in front of me. Needy and waiting…"

"*Gavin.*"

My name on her lips was barely a breath, but I could hear the need and desire in that whisper.

"Arch up," I said, and she did, using the rails as leverage and lifting her back off the bed. I unhooked the clasps of her bra, groaning at the sight of her freed breasts, and I pushed the bra up until it hung over her head behind a pillow.

She gripped the rails again, her body lifting in my direction as I held her gaze, and then I lowered my mouth onto her taut nipple. Shit. She tasted like sweet vodka and candy. Her lips sucked behind her teeth, her head throwing back, but I reached up and took her chin between my fingers.

"Eyes on me, baby."

Chapter Twelve
Chloe

I needed him to move faster.

I was sure I would climax the moment he moved my underwear. I had nearly came at just being bent over his lap. Each slap had sent a pulse through my core and down into my already throbbing clit.

His mouth was back on my nipple, and I rocked and arched into the sensation as he sucked and squeezed the tautness between his teeth. With one arm beneath me, his other traveled down my side, pausing to grip my hip, my ass, and the thigh of my bent leg. My arms were already starting to ache above my head at his slow pace. Every time his tongue swirled on my nipple, or he teased me, I bucked my hips against his, utterly desperate for that friction.

He chuckled on my skin, tongue flicking at my breast, as the very tips of his fingers slid up my inner thigh. "Is this what you want?" he asked. His breath heated over my wet peak, fingers practically dancing over my pussy.

"Yes," I almost cried.

"Yes, what?" His voice was stern. Commanding. Painstakingly sexy. My open mouth snapped shut at the demand, my inhale jagged, and I met his eyes.

"Please."

The corner of his lip lifted again, and he whispered, "That's right, baby," before returning his full attention to torturing me. His middle finger stilled over my clothed, yet throbbing clit, and I felt a needy breath lead me.

"Gavin..."

"Gods, that's beautiful," he whispered, sucking on my breast again. "Keep saying my name. Every time your greedy little pussy wants more, say my name. Beg for it."

I was going to scream his name if he tortured me like this any longer.

"Please, Gavin," I found myself saying as I lifted my hips toward his hand.

He held my gaze when he finally moved my underwear to the side. His open mouth stilled over my breast, only his tongue dancing over my nipple, and I groaned as I watched that tongue move, felt his finger brush my clit. It was all I could do to contain myself as I imagined that tongue on my pussy and doing the same to my sex.

I strained against the handcuffs, desperate to move my arms and push him between my thighs or thread my fingers in his soft hair—something more than this agonizing tease.

"Taste me," I ground out, chin stretching upward. "Cupid… *Eros*…"

He groaned on my chest before pushing up to kiss me. It was as though those names had made him weak or triggered something inside. He tugged at my thong, and just as I started to pull away from his kiss and tell him to undo the stocking clips, he dug a finger into the lace, and the fabric ripped.

I gasped into his mouth, making him smile against my lips, but before I could say something about him ripping my underwear, he plunged a finger inside me, and every thought evacuated from my mind.

"Fuck, baby," he muttered as he moved to hover over me, his eyes landing on the hand between my legs. He met my gaze again, and my mouth sagged as he inserted a second finger inside me. My eyes rolled with every slow thrust, every press of his thumb on my clit. I lifted my hips eagerly, saying his name again as my walls tightened around him.

"Don't come yet," he told me.

I whimpered in response, my aching arms trembling. "Gavin…"

He thrust his fingers hard inside me, making me wince. "Not yet," he said again as his fingers curled, tantalizingly hitting that spot that felt so fucking good, and my eyes rolled in pleasure. Shit. I was melting in his grasp, willing to plead and cry for more.

"Gods, you're eager for that end," he rasped as I lifted my hips to him. "Say my name again."

His words only made me bite my lip harder. I called out his name once more, back arching into him, and he was smiling wickedly when I finally opened my eyes.

"Do you want me to taste you?" he asked.

I bit my bottom lip and nodded vigorously. "Yes," I said, and just as he opened his mouth, I muttered, "Yes, please, Gavin," before he could say it.

He scoffed, then glanced down at the way the light caught off his soaked fingers when he pulled them out of my pussy, and his lashes lifted to me again as he tasted my glistening juices on his middle finger.

"You beg so well, sweet girl." His pointer finger danced over my lip, his brow arching down at me. "Open your mouth," he said. "Lick yourself off my finger. Taste that sweetness."

I did, and I hummed around that digit, holding his eyes and watching his pupils widen as his tongue darted out over his lips. I ached for his absent touch, and he smiled as if I had just completed his favorite task.

"My perfect girl," he whispered.

I was going to come from just his fucking words.

He kissed the tip of my nose and shifted from over me. I couldn't breathe as he sat up to his knees between my bent legs, anticipation making my clit pulse. His hands stretched on the backs of my thighs, making me hike them into the air, completely exposing my bareness down below, and Gavin groaned as he stared at me.

"Look at you…" he breathed, his thumb trailing dangerously close to my sex. "That pretty little cunt glistening…" His head tilted, lashes lifting, as he grazed that finger over my throbbing clit. I flinched at the touch, and that smirk hiked higher.

"You look like my favorite candy, baby."

The words caught me off guard, breaking me briefly out of my daze, and I felt my brows knit together. "What is your favorite candy?" I asked.

His only reply came in the form of his dropping to his stomach and hoisting my legs over his shoulders. "Do you know what I like to do with my candy?" he asked, his nose nudging against my pussy, his heated breath brushing my sensitivity… It took everything in me not to tighten my thighs around his head and urge him closer.

"What?" I asked with a silent gulp.

His gaze steadied on mine as he placed soft kisses on my inner thigh. "I like to savor it… one lick at a time…" He was toying with me, making my breath hitch every time he looked like he would take me in her mouth. "… until every bit of the hard shell is gone, and that warm center melts in my mouth…"

The right corner of his lips elevated as he kissed my entrance, and then he looked back up at me. "Will you melt for me, baby?"

My jaw was practically trembling as I whispered, "Yes."

That damn smirk met me, and I watched as his nose brushed against my folds, followed by more soft kisses on my thighs… and the first time his tongue licked my clit, I melted into the mattress.

Deliberately, he licked me. Tortured me. Tasted me. *Feasted* on me. Every suck of his lips and stroke of his tongue sent me spiraling. His fingers dug into my ass as he held me there. Fucking hell, I wanted to pull his hair and have him suck on me until my lip bled from holding back that release.

My head threw back when his tongue circled inside. I squirmed and cursed his name every time I was forced to take in a sharp breath. I began to roll against his mouth, my legs starting to shake as my climax crested. His tongue felt as though it were made for me, and I never wanted him to stop.

"Gavin…" I grabbed the rail behind my head, my arms thoroughly numb. A whimper escaped me as I tried to deny myself from coming all over his face.

"Look at me," he said, his lips landing on my thigh. "Watch me while I feast."

I picked my head up and looked down, nearly falling apart at the sight of him pulling my clit into his mouth and sucking, holding my eyes with his. I didn't know how I could possibly get wetter, but I knew I had. He reached up around my body and grasped my breast, squeezing as he gripped my thigh tighter in his other hand. His tongue tortured me in the best way. My heels dug into his back, toes pointing as I yanked on the handcuffs. I needed to grab something—*anything* to help keep my composure.

Another whimper choked from me, and I began to tremble. Tears glistened in my eyes. My entire body seized to the point that I thought I might break—

He slipped a finger inside me, prompting me to buck against his hand as that finger plunged effortlessly in and out of me with his continued tongue tease. I cried out, my arms straining…

"Gavin," I gasped. "Gavin, I'm going to—"

"Not yet, baby," he said. He moved his finger from my pussy and stretched that digit between my cheeks, searching for my other entrance, and when he found it, he whispered that finger over it.

"You wanted me to tease you," he said, a soft chuckle leaving him. "Let me tease you." He kissed my clit, and as he did, he slipped his fingers inside both entrances, and a chill rolled over my skin.

"Oh, god, please," I cried out.

His low laughter sounded, vibrating my entrance, and he shifted deeper inside. I dared to meet his delightedly dark eyes, the smirk on his face.

"That's right, baby," he practically growled, tongue laving over my clit. "Say my true name. Call on your lustful god to bring you to your end."

I didn't care if he was Cupid or Gavin, or Santa, or the fucking tooth fairy.

I was going to scream for him. I would scream for that release.

I jerked against the railing headboard so hard that the bed creaked. I was lost—out of body. "Gavin—"

"Beg for it, Chloe," he demanded as he picked up his pace, his fingers hooking inside me. "Beg your god."

I did.

I pleaded with words I didn't know I was saying. My body quaked down to my core. Every tease from the moments before came crashing down. I picked my hips up off the bed, eagerly moving with his tantalizing strokes.

He sat on the bed and began thrusting his fingers in and out with such vigor that my mind blanked. Pressing his chest to the back of my thigh, he pushed my leg forward and placed his other hand around my throat.

Pleasure ricocheted through me, and a tear fell down my cheek. I was reaching, reaching—*reaching*. I'd never felt my body under such a strain. His fingers on my throat squeezed beneath my jaw, making my vision cloud. A numbing sensation trickled over my skin with a violent tremor.

And when his breath hit my cheek, I couldn't hold myself together any longer.

"Let that pretty pussy rain, sweet girl."

My climax hit me like a slap to the face. I released with a scream. His hand was off my throat and from within me, and before I could even finish coming, his mouth was back between my thighs, and he was feasting on me like I was his last meal.

His tongue lashed inside me, and he drained my juices. Sucking my clit, I convulsed even harder. My legs were a flinching mess, but I could do nothing about his continuing to torture me—didn't *want* him to stop, no matter how much my body might cry for a break. It was pain and desire and greed unlike anything I'd ever known, a worship even, and I kept coming again before I could stop myself. Until I saw spots in my blurring vision, and I nearly began to cry from the overwhelming sensation.

As he finally straightened over me, I tried to catch my breath. I sniffed back my exhaustion and swallowed my tears. I couldn't move, couldn't feel my arms, my legs, or my hands.

Golden light hit the back of his figure, and for a brief second, I thought perhaps I *was* looking at a god.

Chapter Thirteen

Gavin

Gods, she was stunning.

Her moan was a sound I wished I could put on repeat. The look in her eyes as she denied herself, the taste of her cum on my tongue, how her body responded to me… so *fucking* beautiful.

I released her wrists from the handcuffs, knowing her limbs were exhausted from straining, and she limped against the mattress, soft groans leaving her as she continued to come down from that high.

A quiet smile crept on my lips when I picked up my sweater from the floor with the intention of putting it on her.

"Can you hold your arms up for me?" I asked.

"Fuck you," she muttered.

A laugh I barely recognized as my own left me. A genuine laugh. One that didn't feel expected or forced. It warmed my stomach, and another look at her satiated face had that warmth traveling to my already aching cock.

"Right—" I lifted her arms one by one, eventually getting the sweater on her and pulling her soft hair out from the back. As I started to pick her up into my arms, though, she reached for my face and drew me down to her lips.

I took a second, surprised by her actions, but caved into her desperate kiss, dropping her legs back onto the bed and holding her cheek while my other hand entwined in her hair. The kiss nearly sent me back onto the bed with her. Fuck, the things she did with her tongue... My cock was already throbbing from watching her come apart, and this kiss wasn't helping matters.

I knew she needed a break more than my dick needed to be stroked. I wrapped my arm under her knees and picked her up off the bed, then took her into the living room and placed her on the couch. Her eyes closed and she groaned when I released her.

A reality show that I hated admitting I knew a lot about came up on the television screen upon turning it on. It caught my eye for a few minutes. I hadn't seen this episode, but I tore myself away to go to her fridge when the commercial came on. I'd been reading ingredients on the drinks in her fridge earlier when she'd come out of the bedroom, grateful that she had turmeric coconut water in there to stay hydrated.

For a few seconds, I paused at the counter and pressed my hands down to the edges, regaining my breath and trying to force my hardened cock down. I wasn't sure how long she would be out after that, but if she touched me within the next few minutes… fucking gods, I was going to lose it.

Snap out of it. She's just another mortal. Think of terrible things, like your mother—

Gods, if she'd seen me like this, she'd have had a fucking field day. She'd never really enjoyed my antics over the centuries, calling me childish for the pranks and arrows, most especially with one particular exchange with Apollo that still made me laugh.

Oh, the fun that had been.

"Shit."

The sound of Chloe's voice halted my reminiscing. She was sitting up slowly, a haze in her eyes, and muttering, "What just happened?" as she took in her surroundings.

I smiled her way and poured a large amount of coconut water into a cup for her. She was stretching her fingers as if trying to get the feeling to return to them when I reached her. I stilled at the sight of her in my sweater, mascara smudges beneath her eyes, her hair out of place and frizzed in the back from where she'd been laying.

Seeing her there, in all her raw glory, remembering every noise she'd just made, every look of her scrunched-up face, her biting her lips… she was stunning. My stomach twisted at how vulnerable and exposed she was right at that moment, how beautiful it was seeing her in such a bare state.

I extended her the drink without saying a word and then sat on the coffee table in front of her. Her fingers were shaking upon taking the glass, and I bit back my amusement as she gulped the liquid down, holding the cup with two hands. A dribble of water made its way down her chin, one that she didn't bother to wipe off when she relaxed back in the seat, her cup sitting lightly between her bare legs.

I reached for her foot, pulled her calf into my lap, and began massaging it while she collected herself. Her eyes closed, flinching every so often with my kneading fingers, and I thought she might fall asleep right there. But after a few moments, she finally rolled her neck, cracking it, and her heavy eyes opened to meet mine.

My lips dried at her satisfied gaze. "Okay? I managed.

"Great," she replied as she took another sip of her coconut water. "I think I'm still coming. What did you do to me?"

I chuckled under my breath and pulled her other leg into my lap. "Baby, I'm just getting started," I promised.

A small smile rose on those pouting lips as she sat up and took her leg away from me. I reached forward instead and wiped the mascara that had streaked beneath her eyes, and she looked like she might laugh.

"I'm a mess, aren't I?" she asked.

"You're fucking gorgeous," I said without hesitation, barely hearing my own voice.

Our eyes locked, and that knot in my stomach tightened. Her doe eye dilated, a faint blush on her cheeks, and for a split second, I wondered why the compliment seemed to still her.

"What?" I asked.

"Nothing," she said quickly. She looked down at her drink, her hair falling over her face, and with a bite of her lip, she leaned toward the table and grabbed the bag of candy hearts.

"I believe it's your turn," she said, dangling it in front of me. "Choose them while I learn how to walk again."

I chuckled as she rose to her feet, her balance wavering slightly—enough that she grabbed my shoulder as she passed by—and she made her way to the kitchen. I couldn't stop myself from watching her walk and then bend over into the fridge to grab something from the inside.

A string cheese stick.

She grabbed a couple of them, munching on one, and made her way back to the couch as I moved onto the cushions where she had just been sitting.

"Go ahead, Cupid," she teased. "Let's see how you play."

I pulled the first heart from the bag.

MAKE ME CUM

She made an 'ooo' noise, her mouth full, and she sat sideways on her knees beside me. I laid the candy heart on her thigh and pulled out another.

BEND ME OVER

"That one is for me," she said, her arm linking around my neck, nails scratching lightly on my neck. Goosebumps rose on my skin with every scratch. I could barely concentrate on taking another heart out. I had to resist the urge to grab her by the waist and yank her onto my lap.

I forced my hand into that red bag one last time and took out another candy heart.

RIDE ME

"Fuck yes," Chloe muttered. Her hand landed on my inner thigh, her lips brushing my jaw. She slowly stroked my leg before reaching around for my hand and placing it on her thigh. My eyes fluttered at the pressure of her hand through my pants, and with every movement, I squeezed her body tighter.

"You don't want a break?" I asked, noticing her still-trembling thighs.

"I've wanted you inside me since the elevator," she admitted, making the hair on the back of my neck stand. "And I always get what I want—" she shifted, her breath tickling my ear as she whispered, "Even from gods."

I nearly fucking lost it.

She began to place featherlight kisses down my throat. I reached for her neck, tugging slightly on her hair, and she groaned as I pulled her head up so she was directly before me. I watched as her eyes rolled. A quiet 'ah' escaped her parted lips when I gripped her hair, and she sucked air behind her teeth, face scrunching with the pressure of my grip. The way she took that pain and fed it to her pleasure had me wild. She leaned forward, her teeth grazing my lip, and then she pushed up to her knees, throwing her leg across my waist.

Urgency fueled our kiss. My mouth moved down her throat, sucking and biting her skin as her breasts rocked against my bare chest. She was already grinding on my thighs and holding my head in the crook of her neck. I grabbed the bottom of the sweater and yanked it over her head, barely taking a second to take in the look of her ready and sitting over my lap before I captured her breast in my mouth.

She groaned out my name, nails scratching my neck, and I devoured her soft tits. Gods, they were perfection. I hardly had a few moments to appreciate them before she pulled my head back to her lips. Her hands fumbled on my belt. I gave her ass a hard smack and said, "Sit up on your knees for me," against her mouth. She did, and I turned my attention back to her breasts, distracting her as I shuffled my pants off. My stiff cock bobbed upon its freedom, and as she sat back on my knees, she grasped my dick with both hands.

"Fuck, baby," I muttered. I slapped her ass with both hands hard enough that she winced. Again and again, I spanked her, and each time, she inhaled a sharp gasp of pleasure.

I chuckled into her neck. "My sweet girl likes her ass red, doesn't she?" I said as I fisted her soft flesh.

Her grip tightened around my cock in response, making me curse her name, and her own smile spread as she said, "Don't stop."

Her hips rocked against my dick. Whenever she stroked me, I had to resist taking her too quickly. She squeezed my tip, precum spilling over, and my hands tightened even more on her ass in response. That plump bottom lip sagged as she moaned. I leaned forward, tugging that lip between my teeth, and she turned the motion into a biting kiss that made me pull her flush to his chest.

She was consuming. I was lost in this, in *her*. Her wetness grazed my throbbing cock. My moan drowned into her mouth at the sensation, but it was too short-lived. I sat stunned as I watched her pull away, push off my lap, and then drop to her knees on the floor.

Those fucking eyes stared dangerously up at me as she raked her hands up and down my bare thighs.

"I didn't get to watch you in the car," she said in a tantalizing tone.

I caught a mouth-watering glimpse of her ass and cursed under my breath at the compelling way her skin was prickled red from my slaps. Fuck, the sight had my own skin tingling.

I had made her ass red.

I had marked her flesh and claimed her.

And she…

She had responded *so fucking perfectly.*

I couldn't wait to mark her more.

I tore my eyes away from that masterpiece and looked back at her face. She pushed her hand through her hair and pulled it over her right shoulder, exposing her neck as she leaned up. And when her tongue touched the tip of my dick, I swallowed and closed my eyes.

"Eyes on me… *Eros.*"

I huffed a laugh that turned into a cursing groan when her lips wrapped around me. She tongued my slit, making my stomach knot again. "That's right, baby," I gritted out, fisting the edges of the cushions.

I pushed my hips toward her as she lowered herself. That familiar wet heat surrounded my dick. Fuck.

"Take me deeper, baby," I whispered, wrapping my hand behind her head and giving her roots a gentle tug. I pushed her scalp and watched as my cock disappeared almost entirely into her mouth. I gave her another nudge, feeling her choke. "Shit—that's it—"

I didn't know how long I'd be able to last being able to see her this time. I released the tension on her hair and grabbed the couch instead, allowing her to set her own pace, occasionally thrusting my hips and forcing her to take me all the way.

Every time I watched her bob down, my cock slick with her puckered lips, I fell a little further for her. She pushed her breasts around my cock and bounced a few times up and down. Gods, the sight of my dick being wrapped with those perfect tits… I strained to hold my composure. Precum spilled over my tip and dripped onto the pillow of her breast, and when she licked it up and swirled that tongue on my head again, those bright eyes widening up at me, I had to reach for her head again.

"You're a dirty girl, aren't you? You want me to fuck that mouth?"

The hum that vibrated around my cock in response was enough to make me fist her hair tighter.

"Yeah, you do," I rasped. "Open wide. Let your god have you."

I lifted my hips and held her steady as my cock moved deep in and out of her mouth, watched her salivate around me and gag with every thrust. She drew her lips tight, trying to keep up with my movements, and I strained at seeing her hollowed cheeks, feeling her nails scratching my thighs.

She was so fucking magical; it took everything in me to stop. I was done for if she continued, so I forced myself to sit up and pull her mouth off, then captured her lips with mine.

I had to know how wet she was after sucking me off, if she was as wet as she'd been after she'd drowned in my cum in the car. I reached between her thighs and—*fucking gods.*

"Gods, you're drenching again," I hissed. "Is this just from sucking my cock? Do you want it that badly?"

"Yes." She wrapped her fingers around my length, her thumb swirling on the slit. "I want you inside me."

Those words surged me. I took her lip between her teeth again, biting and holding her eyes with mine until she winced. I wrapped my hand around the back of her head and whispered, "Ride me," upon letting her go.

Her lips crashed into mine again, and as she stood, I wrapped my hands to her ass and gave her another hard spank, prompting her to moan into my mouth. Our kiss was furious and messy—tongues lashing, her hands holding and tugging my hair like she meant to imprint her grip into my mind. She sank over my thighs, one leg at a time, before pushing her clit against the tip of my length.

I leaned forward to suck her nipple into my mouth before muttering, "Please tell me you're on birth control," and I settled my chin on her breasts as I looked up at her with pleading eyes.

A soft laugh escaped her as she pushed the hair on my forehead back. "I wouldn't have invited you back here if I wasn't," she said.

Relief swept through me. Gods, she was cute. That little laugh… fuck. I wondered if she knew what that laugh and coy smile did to me. I kissed her between her breasts and then bit that pillow, making her suck in a sharp breath.

She rose up on her knees again and rocked against the tip of my cock. "Are you ready to come for me?" she asked.

I inhaled deeply, forcing myself to calm at her tease, and I tipped her chin back with my knuckle. "No, baby," I said as I positioned myself at her entrance. "You're going to use me."

Chloe's brow raised, her hips continuing to rock tantalizingly against my dick. "Am I?" she asked in a breath.

"I can get off at the mere sight of you," I said. "I want you pleasured." I shifted slowly beneath her, using my hands to spread her cheeks and hold her ass at a hover as I deliberately began sliding my hips up and down, barely pushing inside her drenching entrance.

"Use me, sweet girl," I breathed out. "Take your pleasure. Let that greedy little pussy feed."

Her lips slammed into mine again, recklessly, and my entire body caved when she sank onto me. I cursed at her tightness around me, at how it stretched and molded to allow me in. She shifted atop me, working herself in slow movements, until finally her pussy took the whole of me in.

Shit. I grasped her hips tighter, holding myself back from creating a rhythm for her. She was so tight around me. Wet and consuming. Fuck, she was perfect. The way her breasts pushed up between her arms and fit against my chest, how her flesh melted in my hands. I squeezed her again, muttering out her name and aching at denying my release. Gods, I could have let myself go so easily. Just seeing her atop me would have been enough. She felt so fucking amazing, and every time that little sharp gasp escaped her, I had to grit my teeth.

Her shoulders tensed up, mouth open, jaw quivering… "Fuck, right there," she whimpered, her hands bracing on my forearms. She leaned back a little, adjusted herself, and a higher-pitched moan sounded from her. My nails dug so deep into her skin that I was sure she would have half-moon bruises left behind.

"That's it," I said as I watched that pleasure spread over her beautiful face. "That's my girl," I breathed. "Give that cunt what she wants."

It took everything in me not to throw her onto the couch and haul her legs in the air, finish fucking her in a manner that would have had her pleading for her god again. But I held onto those hips instead. I sucked her breast. I cursed on her skin and squeezed her ass, letting her find that sweet spot inside her. She could use me for everything and anything she wanted. Because watching her face and seeing her take it had me rock hard and begging. I could have watched her like that for hours.

She threw her hands around my face and kissed me, her movements becoming faster and faster. I could feel her walls tightening, noticed her breaths turn to gasps, and as she reached that edge and started to cry out into my mouth—

I pushed her back, grabbed her around the throat with my right hand, and slapped her ass so hard with the other that she startled aloud. Her entire body jerked, her mouth agape as she tried to cry out, and I held her there.

"Don't move," I whispered.

I watched her eyes widen as I squeezed her throat and began to rail inside her. She braced her hands on my knees behind her, surrendering wholly to me. I felt her walls convulsing, saw the tremor over her body, and when she came… fucking gods, she came. My cock glistened with her release with every deep thrust. *Gorgeous.* I forced my gaze back to her face, seeing her eyes roll, her mouth open as she gasped for breath. I slapped her ass harder, and with her nails digging into my chest, I, too, came crashing down.

I spilled inside her and released her neck, grasping her forearms and pulling her torso against mine, and as she limped into my arms, she kissed me with stolen breaths.

Shit. I couldn't move, and it seemed neither could she. We were both shaking with the letdown of what had just happened between us. I held her against my chest as we settled, as my cock finished twitching inside her, and when she pulled back and met my eyes, I couldn't stop myself from kissing her softly.

This woman…

"I should… I should go clean up," she whispered after a few more seconds.

I nodded, my chest still heaving against hers. As she slipped off of me, I caught myself staring at our combined juices on my cock and then spilled over the stretch marks on her inner thigh. A low groan left me at the sight of it.

So fucking beautiful.

Every movement in the bathroom made my body ache.

And I couldn't stop smiling about it.

Fucking hell. I hadn't been satisfied like that in… well… ever. We weren't even finished yet.

However, I was done with this particular lingerie. The stocking clips were starting to dig into my legs, and I was sure there were marks in my skin from the scrappy belt.

It was snowing again when I looked out the window from my bedroom. Having grown up where I didn't get to see snow often, I couldn't help but admire it for a few moments. I could practically feel the chill of it on my skin despite the warmth of my rustic apartment.

My phone lit up in my bag by the table where Gavin had left it, illuminating the inside of my purse and the brick wall behind it. I realized that this was probably the longest I'd ever gone without looking at it to check emails or text messages. I shuffled out of the lingerie before grabbing my phone off the nightstand.

Having fun?

Lana.

I smiled at the screen and replied back.

Did you make it home safe? I asked.

Just got here, she said. *Wanted to make sure the serial killer hadn't driven away with you into the night.*

I laughed. **I'm not dead yet. No promises. You might find my body in the morning though.**

I'll check in before work.

See you tomorrow, Clo. Have fun ;-)

I hope he's doing everything to you from those filthy books.

Well, he's not a demon. But I can't be picky, I joked.

LMAO! Clo!

He swears he's a god. Eros, to be exact. Cupid!

Is he? she asked.

I haven't decided. Maybe

Damn girl. You found a god?

I need to hear this. Save me details

I'll see you tomorrow, I texted. **Ice cream time.**

Lol the essential between fucks snack, she replied.

Obviously. Who did you take home? I asked.

Total loss :-(that's okay. I can take care of myself.

What about the last one? David?

Too drunk to function.

I'd had too many of those in the past to count. **Ouch**

Exactly.

See you tomorrow, Clo. Enjoy your god ;-)

Night, Lan

I closed the phone and went to my dresser, intent on finding something a little more comfortable, yet still sexy. I finally decided on a pair of lace, high-waisted cheeky panties and a matching balconette bralette. It was the only bralette I'd ever been able to find that genuinely fit my breasts, and I loved it. I put on fuzzy socks as I grabbed a bottle of water from the nightstand, and then I made my way back into the living room to see what Gavin was up to.

He was still on the couch, though he'd put his skinny dark jeans on again and was drinking the rest of that coconut water while watching whatever reality TV had popped up on the television.

His music was still playing on the speakers—softer— but I could see him moving his head to its beat as he watched the show. He was so sexy sitting there on the black couch, the brick wall behind him seeming to highlight his dark ginger hair. The only lights coming in were from the neon signs across the street, the lights from the other buildings and down below, and from the TV. He must have shut off the kitchen light when he grabbed a drink from the fridge.

I smirked at the sight of him seeming so at ease there, and as I cracked the lid on my water, I leaned sideways against the door frame. I couldn't wait for him to spin me around and rail me from behind—preferably with my hands tied behind me, one leg in the air, his hand in my hair or around my throat and pulling me backwards while he spanked—

Calm down, Chloe.

"Cats or dogs?" I asked, and Gavin finally looked my way.

His gaze darted wholly over me, and it was clear he hadn't been paying attention to what I said. I shifted beneath that stare, feeling like he might rise from that chair and scoop me off the floor again.

"What?"

Chapter Fifteen

Gavin

"Cats or dogs," she repeated.

I had to adjust myself as she stalked my way. Shit, this outfit was even hotter. Then again, at this point, I was sure she could make trash look sexy.

"Ah… dogs," I replied upon her reaching me.

She reached onto the couch and grabbed my sweater, and when she leaned over, she paused at my face, smiling widely before kissing me in a lingering manner. Were I not trying to recover from our previous bout, I would have pulled her onto the couch again and taken every liberty with that body of hers.

She pushed my sweater over her head and then straightened to go back into the kitchen. I playfully grabbed her ass as she left, making her jerk; a quiet laugh escaped her lips, though she kept going. I leaned back and watched her walk, allowing my gaze to travel over her pear-shaped ass, watching it jiggle as she opened the fridge. I was ready to watch it shake across my lap or from behind as I slammed into her.

Patience, I told myself.

"Car that you would give your right testicle for?" she called out as she bent to peer into the freezer.

"No, not the right one," I said, grabbing my chest. "That's my favorite."

She lifted a brow at me over the freezer door, and I scoffed.

"Black 67' Chevelle," I answered.

Her lips puckered, making an "ooo" sound as she emerged from the freezer with a pint of ice cream. "Had to be the sixty-seven, though."

"Would be the 69'—"

"If it wasn't for that damn nose," she finished, grinning widely.

I chuckled under my breath, surprised that she knew the car at all, and I was even more curious about the ice cream in her hand. Although, as I continued to watch her, I couldn't help playing along with her questions.

"Job at sixteen," I asked.

"Veterinary tech," she answered. "Ruined my entire desire for the field." She grabbed a spoon from the kitchen drawer. "Ice cream?" she asked, holding up a spoon.

I mockingly rubbed my abs and slumped further into the couch, legs widening. "Surprised you have to ask after that round."

Her smirk widened. "I hope you're not completely exhausted. We still have quite a few hearts to get through," she said. "What was it you said at the bar? That you had planned on doing each of these to me? One by one?"

I ran a hand through my hair. The bar had felt like a lifetime ago. "My plans haven't changed," I promised.

She closed the drawer with her hip and left the lid to the ice cream on the counter before making her way over to me again. "I have a bad habit of eating ice cream on nights that I'm up late," she said as she crawled onto the couch at my side. "Mostly leading up to the holidays. Big sales and all. Everyone needs a graphic for every little thing." She licked a heaping mound of ice cream off the spoon. "It's the fucking worst," she said with a full mouth.

I chuckled at her, and she dug another heaping teaspoon out, then held it for me to eat. "Ice cream and reality tv," I said as I leaned forward and licked the cookies and cream flavor. "Shit habit of mine as well."

"God, doesn't it make you feel better about yourself?" And the brutal honesty of her tongue made me laugh. She sighed back against the cushion. "This is the first night since last summer that I haven't been buried behind my computer," she admitted. Her head rolled and she looked me over. "You're a terrible distraction."

My smile broadened. "Distraction is something I'm good at."

She shook her head, took another bite of ice cream, and turned her attention to the tv. I grabbed the other spoon she'd brought over and sat up, digging out a spoonful of ice cream for myself.

"What is it that you do?" I asked.

"I'm a graphic designer," she replied. "Freelance work. I have a lot of clients around the states. I do all my work from home. I get to travel occasionally, so that's fun—oh wait, I love when she does this—"

I almost laughed as she mimicked a scene from the show, having seen the woman on TV make a particular gesture before. Chloe sank back into my side then, curling herself beneath my outstretched arm.

"What about you? What does the *god of desire* do in his free time?" Her eyes comically locked on me. "Or does he have a day job?"

"He has a day job," I replied. "I'm an app developer."

"Oh? Anything I've heard of?"

Besides the most popular dating app out? No.

But I resisted telling her.

"Maybe," I shrugged.

She snickered. "So, you're mysterious now?" she teased. "You're not ready to divulge all your secrets to me?"

"Give me another round," I joked. "Then we'll talk."

"You know what we should do," she said, and I squinted at the look on her face.

"What's that?"

"First, we should order pizza," she said. "There's a place downstairs that delivers up at all hours of the night. And second, we should leave a bowl on my balcony to catch some of this snow. It's coming down pretty hard. We'd have enough for snow cream in an hour."

"What is snow cream?"

Her eyes widened as though I'd just uttered the worst thing I could have possibly said. "What—you don't know—oh, this is a *tragedy*."

She was on her feet in a second, the ice cream forgotten about, and she retrieved a silver bowl from beneath her cabinet. I started to ask what she was going on about as she reached me again, but she just grabbed my hand and pulled me out onto the fire escape landing before I could.

Snow circled her as though her gravity were pulling it in. She placed that silver bowl on the step, and then treaded up to the banister.

I beamed at her there—her head thrown back, my sweater hiked above her lace underwear as she held her arms wide, that carefree look on her face as she stuck her tongue out and the snow landed on her…

I took my phone out and snapped a photo of her.

"What's the name of your pizza place?" I asked her.

She moved to my side, huddling against me for warmth, and I let her type it in my phone. She had the order ready for payment within a couple of minutes, and I just laughed when she offered to pay.

"Never happening," I said, snatching the phone away. I entered the last three digits of my card for security, and the confirmation screen popped up. "Thirty minutes," I told her.

She gazed at me with a coy smile that made me want to kiss her again.

"Thirty minutes… whatever will we do to occupy the time?" she asked with a bat of her lashes.

I leaned forward and trapped her between my body and the iron banister, my hands bracing onto the railing on either side of her. Her leg bent around me as she smiled.

That *fucking* smile.

Gods, where had she come from? How was I in such need of her?

I tried to contain the swell of desire rising from the pit of my stomach as I stood there. It was an insatiable craving, a rush of adrenaline just being near her. I had to keep myself together.

"I suppose we'll just sit around and watch more of your reality TV," I said with a shrug.

"You say that as though you wouldn't enjoy it," and the way she laughed then made my stomach knot.

"I have another suggestion," I said.

"What's that?"

I gravitated forward, brushing my nose against her cheek. Her mouth opened as her palms settled on my bare chest, eyes darting from my lips to my eyes, and just as our lips grazed, I said in a breathy tone, "Tell me about this snow cream."

An unexpected snort left her, causing her to clap her hand over her mouth, and she laughed heartily. "And here I thought you were being broody," she jested.

"I can be broody," I said, committing the sound of that laugh to memory. "But you have me very interested in why we're collecting filthy snow in a bowl."

"It's something my family always did," she said. "We used to sit the bowls on our cars when the snows came because we only ever got snow every few years. But you can't collect it from the ground. You have to let it get in the bowl like this. I learned that the hard way. You take the snow and mix it with sugar and condensed milk. It has to be the right amount, however. Otherwise it turns to mush, and ice cream makers help out a lot, but... we would just mix it in a bowl."

There was a glisten in her eyes that I didn't quite understand, and I wondered why the mention of it had made her sad when she'd been so excited only moments before.

"My dad used to bring home a can of that milk any time the forecast even mentioned snow... No matter how late he had to stay out on call, even in the middle of a storm... He always brought it home for us." She sighed heavily and looked up, letting the soft flakes hit her cheeks for a long moment, and I reached a hand beneath her shirt to squeeze her waist.

"Shit," she muttered, blinking fast. "Anyway," she continued, seeming to compose herself. A smile flashed on her lips, her hands slapping softly on my chest, and her lashes lifted. "It's a good thing I grabbed a can at the store yesterday," she added, and I knew she was deflecting from whatever it was that had just bothered her.

"Now, I get to show you what you've been missing out on all your life," she finished.

"I think I've been missing out on a lot," I said, deciding not to push the subject. "I mean, polluted snow sounds extremely appetizing—"

She smacked my chest, and I laughed aloud, swinging back slightly as I held onto the railing.

"—Especially the snow that you clearly scooped off the ground," I continued. "We should try that now—"

Her mouth agape, she picked up some of the collected snow from the rail and threw it at my face. But as she bent out of my grasp, I pulled her back in, my lips crashing down on hers.

It was smiling and laughter that lingered between us and that kiss. We swayed beneath the falling flakes, holding on in a moment that seemed to lull. I could taste the cold on her skin, the water on her chilled throat when I kissed down her neck. The laughter faded, leaving behind kisses and soft sucks of breath from her in my ear, making chills rise on my skin—and not from the cold, but rather from the allure of her noises. Her nails scratched the back of my head as she held me in her neck, and she leaned back over the railing.

I grabbed her ass and lifted her to sit on the banister. Her thighs went stiff, a squeal left her, and she hugged her arms around my neck.

"Gavin!"

"I got you, baby," I promised.

Snowflakes melted on her face as my hand landed on her cheek. I took another few seconds to admire her as a soft wind blew through her damp hair and brushed over our bodies. Her cheeks were rosy from the chill, brown eyes and pale skin bright against the illuminated night surrounding us. We were the only ones awake, the only ones with lights radiating through that darkness.

The city was asleep, but we were aflame.

With that soft smile on her lips, she leaned forward to kiss me again. Slower this time, the cold around us barely apparent with the heat rushing through our veins. I slid my hands beneath the sweater to grasp her tighter, deepening our kiss. The lust between us heightened with every sweep of our tongues, to the point that I couldn't get her close enough. All space vanished between our bodies, and yet, I needed her more. I craved her. No games…

This woman.

And when I finally moved my hand and pushed a finger between her thighs to her warmth, I decided how I would survive this chill.

"Hold the rail and raise your ass," I said, pulling back.

"What—"

I kissed her hard and moved her hands myself, pressing them onto the cold banister. She sucked that pouting lip behind her teeth again when our mouths parted, holding my gaze as I moved my hands to the top of her underwear.

"Squeeze your thighs around me and lift," I said.

She did, and I pulled her underwear down over her bent knees, but stopped upon noticing how she was squeezing her toes around the rails to hang on. I chuckled under my breath and grabbed her knee. "Unhook this," I said, playfully shaking her leg.

"Gavin, I'm going to fall—"

"I have you," I promised as I stroked her calf. "I'm not letting you go."

And there was something about that statement that wove the knot back into my stomach.

She seemed to consider the words as I held onto her other leg, and finally, with her arms straining, she unhooked her toes. My smile widened, and I leaned in to kiss her pink nose, pulling her underwear off her foot as I did.

"That's my girl," I rasped. "Other leg, baby."

I stuffed her underwear in my back pocket as I kissed her again, squeezing her legs and rubbing them up and down, reassuring her of my intentions before pressing any further. Her cold fingers scratched my jaw, palms lying against my cheeks. I trailed my hand between her thighs again. Her warm, wet center met my fingers, and I groaned into her mouth.

"Gavin…"

My name was a whisper on her tongue. My lips moved to her neck as I became more eager for her. I had to taste her again. I *needed* to taste her again. I wanted to bury my face in that heat and feel her hands in my hair as she dangled on the edge of disaster. I needed to feel her pulse and her legs jump every time she waved off balance on that rail. I could feel her trembling, and I wasn't sure whether it was from the chill or the danger.

I lowered to my knees, ignoring the cold ground through my pants, and I held onto her legs the entire time, making sure she knew that I had her, that I would never let her fall. She flinched when I knelt before her, grabbing my hair and pulling it, jerking my head upward. Our eyes never parted as I moved her thighs over my shoulders and held onto their outsides.

There was a questioning in her gaze, and I could see the thrilling fear suddenly present in her dilated pupils.

"Squeeze your legs around me—" Her bent legs stiffened, knees bending over my shoulders and her calves wrapping beneath my armpits, "—just like that… Hold onto the railing or my hair. You're doing so well, baby."

Her eyes fluttered as I leaned in to kiss each of her thighs.

"Don't let me fall," she whispered.

I smiled, my hands gripping the tops of her thighs. The vulnerability in her eyes, the snow coming down and landing in her hair, the streetlamps and neon red lights behind her… I found myself retracting my previous statement of how I'd seen her at her most beautiful state.

"I have you," I said. "You're all mine."

Our eyes stayed locked as I shifted forward, and with my first kiss on her clit, her shoulders limped, and her hands relaxed just slightly in my hair.

Every stroke of my tongue made her moan, and I memorized her twitches, her sounds, and her taste. After a few moments of her audible satisfaction sounding in the quiet night, I wondered if she forgot she was sitting on two inches of railing, outside with the neighbors just a few feet away.

I chuckled against her, sucking her clit into my mouth and making her gasp, and she cried out my name.

"That's right, baby," I said between tortures. "Tell your neighbors who you belong to."

She cursed the air, her voice a little softer this time, but she didn't tell me to stop. Her grip tightened in my hair, her breaths becoming shorter and shorter. She was trying to move her hips, but one hand shot to the railing as she seemingly remembered where she was.

Her jaw dropped, and I watched her face scrunch in that beautiful way that I liked—that I *knew*… I teased her with my tongue, in and out, savoring that wetness and heat against my face. She was getting close, her thighs so tense around my head that she was beginning to squeeze my face. Her whimpering was music to my ears.

"Fuck—Gavin—I'm going to—"

She didn't even get the words out before her hands clenched in my hair and her thighs secured so much around my face that I couldn't breathe. Though, I didn't give two fucks. She was spilling on my tongue, and I drank her like I was starving.

My knees were soaked and numb. She continued to quake when I held her legs and pushed back up to my feet. There was a familiar daze in her eyes, as though she was under some kind of trance, and she threw her arms around my neck, her lips slamming into mine.

The kiss was desperate, needing, encompassing. I slipped my arms around her waist, finding her skin soaking with the precipitation coming through the sweater. An ache pulsed from my heart down to my twitching cock.

I curled a hand around her freezing cheek and pushed her damp hair back when we parted. She was spent, and I couldn't get over how with every passing moment, she became even more gorgeous.

"Shower," I managed, though the word seemed to choke out of me.

Her short nails grazed my cheeks, a smile fluttering her lips, and she huffed out a laugh.

"Hot shower would be amazing."

Getting back into the apartment was a stumble.

Chills cascaded over my skin from the freezing snow, heightened by the lingering orgasm and the pleasure still pulsing through me. My heart continued to pound. My toes, fingers, and nose were completely numb.

But I couldn't stop kissing him.

I wrapped my legs around his waist, and he carried me inside. He stumbled over the plant on the floor just inside the window, catching his balance just before we went tumbling down. The warmth of the living room hit my skin as he let me down off his waist, his hand pressing to my cheek. His kisses were long yet needy. I needed to feel his bare skin against mine again, wanted that hot shower raining over us as he took me against the wall or bent me backwards.

Barely parting, I reached for the hem of my shirt and pulled it over my head. His breath whispered against my wet skin, warming me with every kiss down my throat. I tripped on the coffee table when his lips met mine again, but he caught me by the waist. Soft chuckles left both of us as we paused for a moment and swayed together. I lifted to my toes, our noses nudging playfully, and he grabbed my ass, squeezing it enough to make me suck in a sharp breath.

"You like when I do that, don't you?" he whispered.

My fingers curled against his chest when he pinched my skin, and I leaned forward, pulling his bottom lip between my teeth with a tug. "Don't stop," I said.

And he didn't.

Every inch of his hands on my flesh had my chilled body vibrating back to life. I couldn't decide if I loved or hated the erratic pace of my aching heart and the way it seemed to burn my ears and chest, how my muscles felt restless from his every touch, and the way I couldn't seem to get him close enough.

Damn him for making me feel this way.

But, fuck... *Fuck*, it felt good to be wanted.

I reached for the button on his drenched pants, not daring to break our kiss, and together, we pulled them down. His stiffening cock bobbed free, hitting my abdomen before he bent over to try and finish taking off his jeans, fumbling with the bottoms. My bralette was flung off. I grabbed his face and kissed him again, steadying him, and when he kicked his wet jeans to the side, he finally grabbed and lifted me onto his waist again.

Bare skin flush, we slowed as if the contact alone had electrified our connected souls. His hands massaged my ass, making me buck against him with every squeeze and smack. I could feel his hard cock grazing my entrance as he moved with me toward the bedroom. I didn't know, nor did I care, how he knew where he was going with us attached like this, but he side-stepped the coffee table and was nearly at the bedroom door when my doorbell rang.

It was as though that fucking chime doused our minds back into reality. Gavin cursed under his breath as he pulled away from my lips, and I slid down his body to my feet. He rested his forehead against mine, swallowing as he regained his breath.

"Turn on that water for us," he whispered. "Get ready for me."

He slapped my ass as I turned away and headed into the bathroom. I had to remind myself to breathe as I went in. My mind was a jumble of arousal, confusion, and greed. I paced once in a circle as I tried to remember what I was doing.

Shower.

Reality swept briefly over me as I turned on the overhead shower and removable shower head, the cold water drenching my fingers. I willed my breaths to level, closing my eyes and holding the glass door handle for a moment to try and collect myself. Steam began to billow from the water, and I reached out to touch it just as I heard the door snap closed.

Gavin had paused, his hand still on the door, and I straightened as I remembered why he had parted from me to begin with.

"Did the pizza guy enjoy this view?" I asked, looking over his naked body and landing on his stiffening cock. My thighs squeezed at the sight of him again, staring at the trail of his ginger curls below his abs, the heave of his stomach, and the appearance of those straining veins beneath his forearm tattoos.

And it was *such* a nice cock, too.

A devious smirk flinched his lips, and he slowly began to stroke his dick. "Asked if he could join in," he said in a low tone.

"I hope you gave him an extra tip and told him he could stay to listen for my screams outside the door if he wanted," I said.

Gavin scoffed as he walked toward me. "Baby, you're going to scream loud enough he'll hear you in his shop downstairs."

"Sounds a little far-fetched."

"It's a promise."

His arms wrapped around me, and he dipped low, his kiss evacuating the breath that had just tried to enter my lungs. He began walking us backward into the black-tiled shower, and once inside, the heated water rained over our heads, goosebumps erupting on my skin.

He was over me, aggressive hands worshiping me like it was their job. Teasing my taut, sensitive nipples and grabbing my breasts as he kissed from my neck to my collar, lapping up the water trailing down my chest.

I surrendered, losing all fight and nearly going limp as I allowed him to take me—to flip me and press my chest into the steamed wall, his hand moving around my hip to my center. His hard dick rubbed between my thighs as his other hand slid up to the back of my head, his long fingers massaging and gripping at the roots of my hair just tight enough to make my mouth sag. My head sank into him as he held me, and as his chest pressed hard against my back, I felt his smile curl on my neck.

"Give me this," he whispered as his finger dipped inside me. "Tell me you're mine."

That digit swirled over my aching clit, prompting me to lift my foot onto the bench to give him greater access. His grip secured in my hair as I leaned back and reached up behind his neck, my other hand going to his between my thighs. I guided his hand over my clit a moment, making him press and swirl harder over those sensitive nerves before moving to his cock. He was so close to my pussy that I ground my hips toward it, desperate to feel him inside me again. He cursed into my neck, his teeth dragging over my neck, and I answered him.

"Yours," I managed, tilting my chin toward my shoulder. "Take me, Eros. Show me my god."

Every muscle in his body seemed to tense around me. I still wasn't entirely sure I believed him, but I wasn't ruling it out either—not with the way he pleasured me.

He kissed my jaw, his grip tightening on my hip. The hand in my hair drew taut and pulled me back to the point that he had my throat fully exposed, making me gasp, and he whispered in a voice that sounded desperately like a growl, "Put me inside you."

My body jolted as he released my hair, his voice sending a shudder down into my bones. I obeyed without question, and he pressed his flat hand on my back, making me bend lower. His fingers bruised my hips as I moved to slip him inside me. God, he felt good. My pussy seemed to mold around him as though it were only made for him, as though no other man's cock would ever fit as his did.

"Fuck, you're perfect," he muttered as he sank tortuously deep. "Hold that wall, baby. And Chloe?"

"What?" I managed as my hands flattened on the tile.

"Make sure the people downstairs hear you."

I wondered if the people in the building across the street could hear me.

Every thrust had me fighting my weakening muscles. His dick buried deep, hitting that spot and filling me completely. I pushed back on the wall, trying to hold myself steady there, but with the water pounding on my back and numbing my skin, I began to lose myself.

"You scream so well for me, baby," he hissed, and I felt his hand traveling up my spine. Reaching into my hair, he yanked me by the roots, making my body straight and relaxed against his chest as he slowed down.

The heated water spattered over us, misting our bodies as our movements synched. Every time he pushed inside, I fell more into a trance. His breath on my neck. His fingers entwined with mine on my stomach. His lips hit the side of my throat, where he sucked and marked me beneath my hair. I wanted him to leave marks on every inch of my skin, and I was pretty sure that was what he wanted too.

Water splashed in my face as he pulled from within me and flipped me around. I had to grasp his neck and shoulder to keep from falling apart. My back slammed into the tile. He aggressively hitched my legs up and around his waist again and sank his dick deep. He moved his hands to my hips and lifted one thigh higher than the other, encouraging me to shift with him.

"Shit—Gavin—right there." I could hardly talk. My voice was all whimpers and groans. I could feel my edge growing with every deliberate stroke, but I denied that release. My nails dug into his skin, my open mouth catching water as I sank my head back against the wall. His lips were pulling blood to the surface on the pillow of my breast, to the point that a high-pitched gasp left me at the pinch of his mouth. I was swelling around his dick, and he cursed on my skin.

"Not yet," he whispered in a pleading tone.

"Gavin." My muscles staggered as he kissed me, sucking on my tongue and my bottom lip, making me moan into his mouth.

"Not fucking yet, baby," he said. "Fuck, you feel so good."

His lips were back on mine. He wasn't wrong. I didn't want to come yet either. At that point, I never even wanted to feel the cold air on my skin again. Not if it meant I would be absent from this.

I held myself at the precipice longer. His thrusts slowed, and he held one of my thighs higher to push even deeper. His sack hit my ass with a purposeful grind of his hips— *shit*... I was a goner. It was as if he knew exactly the spot he was hitting and how it was making me feel. My toes pointed, legs beginning to shake—

"Gods, you're amazing," he groaned. "Just a little longer, baby."

"I can't—"

His kiss swallowed my words. Tears pricked my eyes from holding myself back. He thrust inside me the deepest he could, and I gasped into his mouth. His pace started picking up, steadily rising and rising. I jerked in his grasp, whimpering, pleading, and ready to succumb at any moment.

"Please," I begged. "Gavin—"

He kissed me again as the tears spilled over my cheeks, and then he whispered, "Let go."

A noise left me that I'd never heard before. My entire body tensed. My nails broke his skin, and I surrendered.

I surrendered and crumbled and came around him. My orgasm spilled over with a vigorous shake. His strokes quickened, and I opened my eyes just in time to watch his face as he came inside me. The look on his face when he came was a sight I wanted to watch over and over. The way his brows scrunched and the deep curse of his moan. As we stilled, our heated bodies rising and falling in unison with one another, I reached out to push his hair back off his forehead, feeling him continue to twitch inside me.

Gavin's forehead met mine as he slid out of me and my feet hit the ground. He pressed his hands into the wall by my head, pinning me there as he continued to calm.

"Who are you," he said in a breath that I almost didn't hear, and I wasn't entirely sure what he meant, nor if I was supposed to know.

So, I simply kissed him and held his face, and he kissed me back with a need unlike the lust he'd kissed me with before.

Gavin continued his slow torture when he finally rubbed me down with soap, making sure to get into every little crevice and cranny of my body, taking eager care with more sensitive places. His lips pressed to every part of me as he doused me in the citrus soap. Bubbles held onto my tender skin, and he treated the soap as if he was painting me—even drawing a bow and arrow on my stomach.

I laughed at his art. "Okay, *Cupid*," I said, grabbing the soap from him. "Let me."

I had never had fun bathing with another person, but I did with him. My hands roamed every part of him, taking special care with his cock. Stroking him back to life and making him groan when I had him hard in my grasp again.

I took the removable shower head down and turned it to the massage setting, then let it beat down at the base of his neck as I pumped his thick cock. Gavin cursed and started to reach for me, but I made him press his hands into the wall and the glass door, even going as far as to threaten him with handcuffs if he tried to touch me. That fucking smirk lifted his lips, but he didn't move as I brought him to his end.

A broad, wicked smile held on my lips at the triumph of his cum shooting over my belly and in my hand. God, he made the best noises when he came. And the look in his eyes when his gaze skated over me after completion had my heart fluttering.

I dragged my finger through the cum on my stomach and locked eyes with him as I licked it off, wrapping my lips around that digit and making sure to suck in my cheeks. My lips puckered as I cleaned the cum off. Gavin looked like he might pounce on me: shoulders tensing, eyes hardening... I wondered how much restraint it was taking for him not to grab me immediately, though he seemed to be patient.

He slowly took the shower wand from my hand as he composed himself, whispering, "Come here," to me before dragging me against his chest.

It was a dangerous command—a challenge—much like when we'd first started our game, and my heart skipped at the way he looked at me. His lips were on mine again, distracting me as he moved that wand over my shoulders and back, down to my hips and the curvature of my ass… And when I felt him move the shower spray between my legs, I flinched out of his grasp.

"Gavin—"

His brow raised, almost as if he knew how powerful that pressure would be against my already sensitive clit. He lifted his chin, a crooked smile rising as he shifted the shower spray to a more gentle setting.

"Let me clean you up," he said.

A laugh escaped me as he teased me with the spray, and before I could get away or open the shower door, he grabbed me by the waist and into his muscular arms again.

"Is this your favorite? Is this what you do when you can't go to sleep?" he mocked, and I grabbed onto his arm, smiling into his shoulder because that was all I could do. My thighs were jelly, and I was beginning to wilt from the pleasure and exhaustion catching up to me.

He sprayed that heavy pressure against my clit again, making me jerk and whimper, and I began to fall apart.

"Do you get in this shower and hold the water on that swollen clit until you can't feel your legs? Do you imagine that shadow, baby? Do you imagine that faceless being while you sit on this bench and pleasure yourself?"

He wasn't wrong, but I didn't have the voice to tell him. I shook as he moved that pressure, hitting me in every place that had tears pricking my eyes. I didn't know how I was supposed to come again. My vision blurred as I started to collapse, but his grip tightened on my waist and held me steady. Thank fuck for his grip. I would have been on the floor without it.

Every time the water moved over my throbbing clit, I jerked in his arms. I hugged his bicep, my open mouth on his shoulder. His name cried out from my lips in a wail, and he steadied the water on my nerves—letting it beat and torture me in the best ways.

Somehow, this was what would be my end. I was sure this was what would send me tumbling in a way that completely numbed my mind and body.

"Let go, baby," he finally said. "Relax for me. I've got you. Give me this orgasm, give me all of you."

I tried to. I wanted to. My heart felt like it might stop as every part of me strained. My weak knees were shaking. I was sure I was drawing blood on his skin from my nails and how I bit his shoulder. But he pulled my chin to him, and he kissed me. And in that kiss, I found surrender. I gave in, letting go of denial.

Wails left me that I wasn't aware that I possessed.

"That's it," he said, and I could feel his muscles tightening around me, his hand clutching my hip like he was holding me up. The water pressure sent my body convulsing—

I crashed. I screamed. I cried out into his collar, my knees finally giving way, but he caught me. He let the shower handle fall and reverberate against the wall as I came crashing down, my body jerking and whimpering, tears springing down from my cheeks. My entire body radiated an ecstasy I'd never felt before. Euphoria swam throughout my every pore, and I wondered how anything else might match the bliss I felt right then.

"There's my sweet girl," he whispered as he kissed my nose. "You did so well, baby."

Chapter Seventeen

Gavin

Chloe nearly collapsed in my arms after I towel-dried her hair. I carried her into the living room and laid her on the couch, placing a pillow under her head. I grabbed one of the blankets from the basket by the television and draped it over her. I didn't eat the pizza, but I did set it out on the table, along with a few more coconut waters and regular waters from the fridge, before then crawling onto the couch by her side and turning on the TV.

I couldn't nap. Even with how tired I was, I continued to stare and wonder about her—how she had come into my life mere hours ago and it had felt as though I'd known her a lifetime, like I'd known her touch and her taste for longer than she'd been alive. The memory seemed to be buried deep within me, but it moved and wove and wrapped itself around my soul, but one look at her sleeping dismissed it from my mind.

The window remained open. I could see where so much snow had collected in her bowl that it was overflowing. A soft chuckle left me, and I started to get up and bring it inside, but Chloe sat up and groaned an unintelligible mutter before I could move. As she shifted to her other side, she hardly looked my way, and she laid her head in my lap like it was her favorite pillow.

The blanket fell to the ground. I reached for it and tugged it up back over her. I moved my hand beneath it when she snuggled against me, moving my fingers absentmindedly while tracing the exposed flesh at the top of her thigh and the bend of her hips. After getting out of the shower, I had put my sweater back on her and the high-waisted underwear, along with a new set of thick fuzzy socks I'd seen hanging out of her dresser drawer.

She was a fucking goddess lying in my lap looking exposed as she was. So vulnerable…

A knot twisted around my heart, and I reached for my phone to check messages in the hopes it would distract me from the feelings racing through me.

Thirty new emails, ten texts—most of which were from my friend, Zayn, asking for details, more notifications from various apps, and finally, tonight's reports on Cupid's Arrow.

I thumbed through the texts and emails quickly before moving to the reports. Everything was up. The party had done a great job exposing more people to the app and helping them find matches.

I closed the reports and instead opened up the app to see what I could toy with. I'd hardly had any time to play other than matching Chloe's friend, Lana, up with a few distractions earlier in the night.

I'd just shifted a fun match together when Chloe stirred atop me.

"How is your lap this comfortable?" she muttered in that breathy voice that sent my hair standing on end.

I squeezed her hip and gave her ass a gentle slap. "Sleep, baby," I told her.

She shifted up at my side and laid her cheek on my shoulder instead. "What are you looking at—are you—" She pulled away and stared at me, suddenly totally awake.

"You're looking at that app when I'm lying basically naked in your lap?"

A tease, but I pondered if perhaps someone had ignored her like that in the past.

"Curses of being a workaholic," I said with a sigh.

"How is that app considered work?" she asked.

"It's my app," I replied.

She nearly balked. "What? What do you mean it's *your* app?"

"It's my app," I shrugged. "I developed it."

And this time she was staring at me like I'd grown another head. "You're *Gavin Erosin?*"

I chuckled lightly. "Does that matter?" I asked.

"You…" She shifted to sit on the edge of the seat, an almost uncomfortable look on her face, and my eyes narrowed.

"What?" he asked.

She blinked as she took it in, and then she slumped her hands in her lap with a soft laugh. "Shit," she finally said. "I could make a lot of money with stories from tonight."

I smiled at the jest in her tone and the delight in her eyes. I never led with my name or, if I could help it, even told some people that part about myself. I liked parading in secret rather than being at the forefront of the brand in the headlines.

"I could see it on the front page of the tabloids while I sat on a yacht and sipped my martini," she continued to tease. "'*Gavin Erosin seduces woman with promises that he is a god.*'" She laughed, and I shook my head. "Too bad I'll never see that headline."

"Why's that?"

"I like having you as my secret more."

There was something about that statement and the look in her eyes that made me want to reach out for her hand and kiss her knuckles. My stomach twisted at how she was smiling at me then,. The light in her eyes was so familiar, though I couldn't place it.

She huffed a quiet chuckle, her hair falling over the side of her face, and I cleared my throat.

"Pizza is getting cold," I managed.

"Oh, I forgot about the pizza." She turned and reached into the box like she was starving. When she slumped back into the couch and took a large bite, her eyes closed, and I knew then just how tired she was from our night.

"Mmm… fuck, this is good—sorry, did you not have any yet?" she asked as she looked over at me.

I smiled and waved her off before reaching for my own slice.

"This show is still going on?" she asked upon seeing what was playing.

"Must be a marathon," I said.

"I love this episode—" she laughed at the antics on the TV, her mouth full, and then reached for the remote to turn up the volume. "Have you seen this one?"

"I haven't," I answered.

"Oh shit—" She was laughing so hard that she moved off-balance, and I couldn't stop staring at her. Eventually, her laughter faded, and on her third slice of pizza, she slumped back into the seat again.

"This pizza is so good," she continued, eyes closing and satisfied noises coming from her. "*So* good."

"If I'd known all it took was pizza to make you orgasm, I'd have taken you to dinner first," I bantered. "Though, I'm not sure we would have made it through the appetizers. I wonder…" I tore off a piece of crust and popped it back, "how long do you think it would have taken the waitresses to notice my fingers sliding in and out of that beautiful wet pussy during dessert?"

"We lasted all the way to dessert?" she asked, brows elevating.

"I think I would have teased you just to see people watch," I said. "I would *love* to see people trying not to get off at the sight of that fucking face you make when you're about to come."

A confident smirk spread wide on her lips. "No, we would have taken dessert to go in your Jeep," she countered. "And I would have ridden backwards on that throbbing cock while you sped down the highway."

"Specific," I said, though the image had me shifting in my seat.

She chewed off another bite of pizza, smiling broadly. "*Every* fantasy… or was that not what you promised me?"

I grinned at my own tease before taking another slice of pizza off the table. "Whatever you desire," I said.

The TV show went on, and together, we laughed. I nearly choked on my food once, and she gave me a hard time about choking, to which I ended up pulling her into my lap. She situated her legs across my lap after a while, and I took up massaging her calves as we sat up to watch shit infomercial TV.

"I don't want to work tomorrow," she said when things got quiet.

"Big projects?" I asked.

"Well… most of my clients are in fashion. Valentine's pretty much marks our launch into spring adverts. It's so weird to switch directly from sweaters and coats into shorts and tanks. But that's the industry here." She leaned on her hand, and I could see a fatigue taking over as she asked, "What about you? Is your office here or do you work remotely?"

"I do much of my work remotely," I answered. "But, my home and office are in California." I dwelt to look her way. "I fly out in the morning."

A heavy sigh left her, and she sat up on her knees. "Can I literally tell you how relieved that makes me?" she asked as she straddled her legs over my lap, our hands entwining together.

"That I don't live here?" I asked, skin tingling at her fingers brushing with mine.

"Yes," she replied. "I didn't want you to think this was going any further than tonight," she admitted. "I work seventy hours a week, mostly in my pajamas at home without showering for days in between," and I laughed at the admission, making her do the same.

A beat of quiet settled there in that room, and I took the few seconds to watch her face soften, a faint blush rise on her cheeks.

"I think you would be an awful distraction from what I want right now," she continued. "And I'm not ready to give that up or put myself in a position that would make it unfair to you."

"Not ready to, or unwilling?"

She paused, her hands toying with mine. "Can I be totally honest with you?"

"I think I can handle that," I said, and she smiled at him in response before sighing so heavily that her shoulders drooped, and she began to rub the insides of her wrist where she had a small raven tattoo on her pulse point.

"After my last relationship, I think I'm utterly terrified that I'll lose myself for someone again," she admitted. "I lost everything about who I had become. It's like this switch just turned off, and I became someone I didn't know. I shut out my family. I stopped talking to friends. And after that relationship ended, I didn't know who to be. I had lost so much during that time that I had nowhere to go and no one to turn to. I fell into this… *hole*. I threw myself into work and everything I could get my hands on. I drank. I cried. I tried things that…" Her voice trailed, a glisten rising in her eyes, and she glanced up at the ceiling.

"And then one day, I looked up, and years had passed." Her voice was shaking, but she just shook her head as she stifled whatever emotion had threatened to surface. "I have worked *so* hard at finding myself again," she said. "I finally got my family back. I found a job that I love that is on my own time… I found reading and nature. A couple of friends who are actual friends and not just pretending… The thought of someone coming in and taking that from me is…" She stared at my shoulder, almost in a trance, exhaling audibly as she continued to brush her thumb over that tattoo.

"I just can't lose myself again," she finally said as she finally met my gaze.

I didn't say anything. I wasn't even sure I was supposed to. So, I continued rubbing her thigh, simply watching her. She laughed softly at herself after a few moments and wiped her cheek.

"You must think I am a complete basket case now," she said.

I chuckled under my breath and cupped her face in my palm. "I think you're real," I whispered.

She covered my hand with her own, holding my eyes. "Tell me why I feel comfortable saying all of this to you when I barely know you," she asked. "Tell me why this is so easy."

I couldn't answer, but it relieved me that I wasn't the only one who felt it.

"Is it your stupid magic?" she asked, amusement in her tone. "Are you using glamour on me?"

A tease, I knew, but I hadn't used my powers on her all night. Everything had simply been us.

"You know what glamour is?" I asked.

"Of course, I know what glamour is," she answered. "I've read Percy Jackson."

I laughed out loud. "The minotaur erotica makes sense now," I said.

She blinked, apparently considering it, her smile widening. "You know, I hadn't thought about that, but I guess it does." Her laugh filled the apartment, and I held onto her as she shook her head at herself. "Oh, isn't it funny the things from your childhood that progress into fetishes and kinks?" Her head tilted, lip sucking behind her teeth, her eyes brightening up at me.

It was so fucking cute that I considered changing my flight the next day.

"I've always found that fascinating," she continued. "How your childhood can mold so much about your life."

Just as she opened her mouth to go on, she sat up suddenly, her wide eyes shooting to the balcony. She bolted off the couch to the fire escape balcony, coming back inside with the heaping bowl of snow after, her face aglow with apparent memories of a childhood she'd loved.

"We have *so* much snow," she declared, making me smile at the look on her face. "Help me make it?"

Helping Chloe make her favorite childhood treat was like stepping into a domestic bliss I'd once forgotten. I leaned back onto the counter while she worked, occasionally helping out with mixing or tasting, and I had to admit, the flavor was enticing. Or maybe it was that the delight on her face was so enthralling that the shit snow could have tasted like my least favorite food, and I would have loved it anyway.

"We have to let it freeze," she said as she bent over to close the freezer drawer, licking her fingers when she straightened.

"Least favorite game as a child?" I asked, continuing our random questions.

"Oh, that's easy," she said as he piled up the dirty spoons. "Duck, duck, goose."

I laughed. "What—why?"

"I was always scared of getting chosen and then having to get up to run or chase someone. I hated it."

"Such a *spoilsport*," I teased.

That smile broadened on her lips. "Accurate," she chuckled. "I used to get so embarrassed. It took me a long time to get over it," she admitted. "One day I just decided, fuck it. I don't care what others think of me. I still don't like public games like that, but… at least now if I trip over my own feet or say something awkward, I know how to own it." She turned to run her cold hands under the water and then leaned back on the counter.

"Favorite holiday—besides Valentine's Day," she added, smirking at me. "Surely the god of desire has another holiday he likes."

"Halloween," I answered.

"Oh? What do you do on Halloween? Dress up with a bow and arrows?"

I eyed her mocking face and shook my head. "Usually working," I answered. "Something about that holiday…" I shifted on my feet, arms wrapping around my chest as I considered why exactly I liked that day. "The entire vibe of it. Its history…"

"The unknown," she added, meeting my eyes. "Dangerous and full of mystery. Dark… It's perfect."

A soft silence padded the room as we watched one another. I shifted the weight on my feet, the question I wanted to ask her dancing on the tip of my tongue. I knew what she had said, but…

"Ideal date?" I asked.

She eyed me. "What a surprise that Sir Eros himself wants to know a girl's ideal date," she mocked. "Shouldn't you know that by all the app data you've collected?"

I scoffed and pulled my phone out to search for her profile. "Your profile is quite literally blank," I said as I turned the phone around. "With the exception of this one photo—"

She laughed at the photo of her eating a cherry. One eye closed like she was laughing, wearing a white tee and her hair down. She shook her head before reaching into the fridge for a drink.

"Do you like ciders?" she asked, pulling two from the inside.

"Are you dodging my question?" I asked.

"I am, yes," she answered, popping the lids off the bottles and handing me one.

My brows lifted as I waited for her answer, staring her down as she avoided it, until she chuckled out loud and rolled her eyes.

"I honestly hate dates," she admitted. "They're so awkward—at least the first few. It's like each one is a job interview."

"What would you prefer instead?" I asked.

"This," she blurted. Her broad smile faltered like she hadn't meant to say it. She uncrossed her ankles and pressed one foot into the bottom cabinet, holding that drink against her chest like she was trying to make herself smaller.

"I prefer this," she continued. "I prefer feeling a connection in person and chasing it."

"What if I took you out?" I asked. "Where would you want to go?"

I knew it was a gamble to even mention it after what she'd admitted about not being ready. She was likely to push me out of the apartment right then, but I was willing to chance it.

She smiled at the floor, her eyes then lifting to mine. "Gavin—"

"Hypothetically," I said before she could completely shut me down. "The romance novel version."

She scoffed and pressed her hand onto the lip of the counter behind her as she seemingly thought it through. "Okay… Ah… Autumn festival or carnival at night," she answered. "With the lights everywhere."

"Weather?"

"Oh, you can control the weather now?" she bantered.

"I might know a guy." A lie, but it was fun to make her think.

"Damp grass and chilling fog weaving through the forest around the outside. Just cold enough that I can wear a sweater and skirt with my boots and hat, and you could wear a sweater and leather jacket—obviously, you have to have the jacket because at some point I would need it—"

"Obviously," I added, my stomach twisting with the vision.

She smiled wide and took another swig of her drink. "We would eat shit fried foods and drink sours and ciders all night. We'd laugh, maybe meet my friends, maybe get lost in the Hall of Mirrors, and you'd spend a ridiculous amount of money on those games trying to impress me."

A short pause rested between us, our eyes locked on one another. I could see what she wanted in my mind, and I was willing to spend whatever she wanted me to.

"What else?" I asked.

She sat her drink on the counter before starting toward me. "You would bribe the Ferris wheel operator to pretend the ride was broken," she continued. "Or to go very slow..."

My chin lifted as she playfully tugged on the belt of my pants, those doe eyes looking up at me. I stared down my nose at her and drifted my fingers along the outskirts of her arms. Lower and lower my hands trailed as goosebumps rose on her skin with every whisper of my touch.

"Excruciatingly slow," I said, one finger toying with the hem of her underwear.

"The other people on the ride would begin to complain," she said. "Perhaps even panic at being stuck."

"Absolute chaos," I said, my fingers trailing lower.

"But we wouldn't know," she whispered as her eyes darted to my lips. "Because your hand would be between my thighs..." Her eyes fluttered as I dipped my fingers beneath the hem on the curve of her ass. "I'd try to be quiet as you teased me, but… in the end, those people would get a show."

"You would sing my name to the stars," I said upon gripping the top of her ass. "That ride wouldn't be the only place you would come for me, though."

"No?"

I shook my head, massaging her ass. Fuck, she was soft. "I'd take you in the shadows between the performer trailers—with my hand over your mouth because the sound of that fucking moan would make people come running. And after I'm done, when your back is raw, and your legs shake, you'll walk around bare… with my cum dripping down your beautiful thighs." Our noses brushed as her hands pressed to my chest, her nails scratching my skin enough to send a chill down my spine.

"I have one condition," she said.

"Anything."

"We get cotton candy before we leave."

I chuckled, swaying with her slightly. "As long as I get to eat it off you when we get home."

Her soft laugh met mine, and I swore a faint blush rose on her cheeks as she stared at her hands for a moment. Tension settled between us—one that made me squeeze her tighter against me. I saw her swallow, and my brows knitted at seeing the nervousness on her face.

"Do you know what I think?" she asked, lashes hitting her eyelids as she lifted her gaze to mine.

I didn't respond immediately. The look in her eyes had me concerned for whatever it was she was about to say.

"What?" I asked.

"I think…" Her eyes darted away, and for a brief second, she stared outside at the snow coming down. "I think I could see myself getting lost again just to have you," she whispered as her eyes met mine once more. "And that scares the shit out of me."

Genuine fear lined her breathless voice, and I leaned forward to rest my forehead on hers.

"I'll find you," I whispered.

Her hands pushed up to my neck, fingers brushing my scruff. "Promise?"

"When you're ready."

Her lips met mine then, and for the briefest of moments, I was there at that carnival. I was standing beneath the night sky with her. I could hear the noise of laughter and screams from the amusement rides. Fog hit my cheeks; a wind circled us. The smells of fresh, damp dirt and pine entered my nose. The taste of cider on her tongue only furthered the vision. It was as vivid as a memory, not a fantasy. So much so that when she pulled back, and I remembered we were just in her apartment, the reality jolted me, my heart skipping.

"What time is your flight tomorrow?" she asked.

I inhaled a deep breath, blinking back at her. "Nine twenty-two," I answered.

"That's very specific," she laughed.

"You asked."

She hugged me a little tighter yet lifted her chin up to see my face. "You'll be gone before sunrise, then," she realized. "You'd better hope this snow cream firms up. You have to taste this before you go."

I chuckled and leaned down to kiss her nose. "I will, baby."

Every time she kissed me, I spiraled further for her, forgetting reality. I grabbed her up behind her thighs and placed her on the counter where I'd just been leaning. Her soft laugh filled my ears as she leaned back, and I started rubbing her thighs.

"What's waiting for you in California?" she asked.

"Top floor condo… the beach… work…"

"Sounds terrible," she mocked.

"The worst."

Chloe reached for my hands. "Do you think we could extend tonight a little longer?" she asked. "You say you're a god. Is there anyone you can call up and ask to stop the sun from rising as quickly as it will?"

I scoffed, thinking of the god I would have to call to make that deal, and I shook my head. "Afraid not."

"I guess I'll settle for your shadow in the dark then," she mused. "What will you settle for?"

I leaned forward, chasing after her as she playfully dodged my kiss, and I ended up burying my face in her neck. She hugged my head there, her nails gently scratching my scalp. I loved the way she did that, how that simple movement made my muscles weak. I didn't know how she did it, and I didn't really care.

"This, here." I placed a gentle kiss on her lips, barely hearing my own voice. "Every thought will be of my good... *sweet*... girl."

She groaned and leaned forward, her teeth scraping my bottom lip. "Call me that again," she murmured. "Tell me I'm your good girl."

I chuckled under my breath. "That's not how it works." I slapped her ass playfully before reaching around her back for the handful of candies I'd left on the counter.

"One more round, baby," I said.

"Tired, Sir Cupid?" she teased.

"Exhausted," I said with a smile. "But I need to feel you around me once more."

I captured her lips in a lingering kiss, her arms circled my neck, and I held her close as I took a handful of the candies in my palm and then held it out to her.

"Close your eyes and pick three," I said, kissing her jaw. "No cheating."

She closed her eyes and stuck her hand into the hearts, and for a final time, she laid the candies on the counter.

GOOD GIRL

"How did that get in there?" I asked, picking it up before she could claim it. I tossed it back over my shoulder, grinning in her face as her mouth dropped.

"What—no, that one counts!" she protested.

Her playful argument made me laugh. I circled my arms fully around her waist, giving her ass another spank. My smile buried in her neck, and I started sucking her throat. Her giggle filled my ears as she laid out another heart.

"Interesting," she said, and I pulled off her neck to see it.

BITE ME

I smiled widely at the heart, delighted at the thought of biting her ass and leaving marks in her skin. She was staring at me when I looked at her again, a soft smirk on her lips, and she tilted her head slightly as she said, "Last one, Eros."

The rasp in her voice tingled down my spine, a restlessness pulling all the way to my extremities. The knot in my stomach tightened to almost pain. That whisper… my true name on her tongue… It was so familiar, and yet…

Whatever it was, it faded the moment our eyes met. She had another handful of hearts in her open palm. I leaned down and chose one with my tongue, and her smile met me when I showed it to her.

"Harder," she whispered.

Goosebumps prickled over my skin. I held her delighted eyes, then asked in a hoarse voice, "Are you ready, baby?"

Chapter Nineteen
Gavin

Taking her into the bedroom, I savored her kiss and every yearning sweep of her tongue. She held me tight, only slowing when I let her go at the edge of the bed and her feet touched the floor. Her sweater was off in a second, both of us fumbling with my pants after. Bare, I whipped her around and held her flush, my hand breezing over her throat, my lips on her neck. Her ass pushed against my stiffening cock, causing more blood to rush there and a fire to ignite in my stomach.

"Are you mine, baby?" I whispered in her ear.

"Yes," she groaned, her arm reaching up and behind my head, fingers gripping my hair.

I moved my hand across her stomach to between her thighs. So wet. So perfect. My other hand tightened around her throat. "When you play with yourself tomorrow, or another man tries to satisfy you, whose name will you call out at your end?" I whispered. "Tell me whose shadow you'll come for."

My teeth raked over her skin, and she moaned out my name.

"Yours," she managed. "Gavin. Cupid. *Eros.*"

Fuck, my cock was throbbing. I groaned against her, trying to hold myself back. But, gods, I needed her. I needed to feel her pussy tightening around my dick. I wanted to hear that moan escaping her like she couldn't stop it.

I whirled her around again and kissed her hard, biting her lip and imprinting on her soul. And when I pulled back, I tugged at the roots of her hair.

"That's my good girl."

Chloe's arms threw around my neck, her desperate kiss landing on my lips, teeth skirting over my tongue as she consumed me. I bent us over onto the bed, leaving her sprawled out on the sheets so I could admire her a moment.

"Bend over for me and grab the rails," I told her.

She kissed me once more before doing what she was told. She turned to her hands and knees, her ass arched in the air, hips greedily moving as her arms lay on the bed, and she grabbed those black bars. My mouth dried at the sight of her so tantalizingly wiggling her ass, as though she knew precisely how fucking much that view would make me wild.

Gods, she was perfect.

"Spread your knees, baby—that's it—" I dragged a finger up her glistening pussy. "You're so fucking perfect," I whispered as I stroked myself and kneeled on the bed. I tapped my cock on her spread cheeks, then spanked her again.

My name groaned from her lips. She moved her hips eagerly toward me. I spread my fingers on her ass and squeezed her softness. Her pussy glistened. Swollen and pink and so fucking ready for me. I sank one finger inside her, cursing at the absolute drenching around that digit. I bent over, kissed her pink ass, and bit the opposite cheek so hard that when I straightened over her again, my teeth mark had indented in her flesh. Fuck, that was beautiful. The indentation. Her wonderful ass.

A groan left her as I dragged my soaked finger over that mark.

"Gavin…" she begged as she shifted to look back at me.

I positioned myself at her entrance and reached down to massage her neck, my tip tickling her cunt. I cursed at how easy it would have been to come all over her ass right there.

"Do you want this?" I asked.

"Please," she whispered as she pushed her hips backward, sliding slightly onto my cock. "Fuck me," she pleaded. "Fuck me like you'll never see me again."

The words, however simple, triggered something inside me. The knot at the pit of my stomach tightened, along with the hand I had in her hair.

I yanked her up by the roots the moment I slammed inside her. She cried out, her head and back bending—*craning*—to my will, and I forced her to look backward up at me. I was buried inside her to the hilt, and as I met her upside-down gaze, her pussy tightened even more around me.

"Careful what you want," I warned, as she whimpered in delight at the grasp I had on her hair.

Her eyes visibly dilated, a smirk twitching on her lips, and she moved her hips in a slow circle. "I want you," she whispered.

My lips met hers, my other hand digging into the bend of her hip, and I began a slow pace. "Hold tight, baby," I told her.

I released her down into the bed, pushing on the small of her back and keeping her bent as I railed into her. The noises her slick pussy made… fuck, she sang for me. That beautiful fucking moan muffled into the mattress, and it killed me that the bed was taking the sound away. I pulled her up by her hair again just to hear her crying out.

"Fuck—*harder*—"

She was going to send me over the edge.

I grabbed and flipped her in one move and lifted her leg so that the backside of her thigh rested on my chest.

I plunged into her again. Again. Again. Her back arched up with every whimper and moan and beg.

"Gavin. I'm going to—"

I thrust deep and stilled a moment, watching her head move side to side, her hands clench on the sheets.

"Fuck... God, right *there*." She gasped and grabbed onto my arm, her mouth sagging.

Goosebumps rose on her skin, and I almost smiled. "Which god, baby?" I whispered as I deliberately pushed in and out, making sure to hit that spot that made her wild. She continued to curse and writhe, the pleasure spreading over her face. I held her ankle on my shoulder and reached to her clit, my thumb swirling over those nerves. She trembled beneath me, her hands shooting to her hair.

"*Eros*—right there—" Another gasp, and she opened her eyes to meet mine, nearly making me lose all concentration at those brown orbs pouring through me. "Shit, you feel so good," she moaned. "Don't stop. *Never* stop."

I had never heard more beautiful words in my life.

She lifted up, grabbed me behind the neck, and kissed me hard. I could feel her body reaching as I set my pace. She was a drug that I wanted to abuse and lose myself in. My forehead rested against hers, the air thickening with our need for one another. She shook, and my heart ached. I wasn't ready to come, not if it meant I might not be inside her again. Her grip tightened on my shoulders, her whimpering sounding beneath me, reacting to every thrust like it was her last moment.

"Don't come yet, baby," I pleaded. "I'm not done with you."

Her neck was exposed with her next moan, and I could tell she was straining to keep herself from spilling over.

"Not yet," I begged.

"I can't," she nearly cried. "I can't. I'm going to—"

"Shit—"

A high-pitched gasp left her. Her walls convulsed in a manner that made all of my muscles tremble. I pulled out of her quickly and flipped her over again, bending her hips to my will, and I buried my cock deep once more. I grabbed her around the waist and hugged her back to my chest, clutching her breast and tickling her clit with my hands. She cursed my name again as the pressure of my moving fingers heightened there.

"With me, sweet girl," I said as I kissed her neck. "Come with me."

She bent forward again, her head lying sideways on the mattress, and I squeezed her body against mine as I took us both to our ends. Another high-pitched wail came from her lips, her hands gripping that sheet so tight that her knuckles whitened, and when she crashed around me, I couldn't keep my own release from spilling over.

The orgasm hit me like an anvil. I groaned out loudly, saying her name and slapping her ass. A cold chill staggered over my entire body—euphoria, like nothing I'd experienced, for her and the satisfied moans coming from her lips.

For a moment, I couldn't move. I spilled completely inside her as her pussy continued to throb around my dick. Shallow breaths sounded in the room with our satiated groans. I didn't want to pull out of her. I could have stayed, kissed her lips and her spine and fucked her again. Slowly, this time, just to savor her one more time.

But I knew she was spent.

I slowly moved out of her, groaning at the sight of my cum dripping out of her swollen, red pussy. Fuck, that was exquisite. I had done that. I had made her scream, cry, beg. I had pushed her body and left prints on her ass, molded this cunt to crave my cock from then on. I dipped my fingers inside her and then spread our combined juices across her ass, making one last crying grunt leave her lips.

"You should see our art, baby," I whispered. "I could fuck you again just to see my cum dripping out of this beautiful cunt."

She twisted onto her back and sat her bent legs on either side of me. A vulnerability stretched over her eyes as she laid there and watched me, her breasts rising and falling with every deep breath.

"I want to watch," she said softly. "When I see you again, I want to see our art. I want to see your cock glistening with what you do to me."

When I see you again.

My stomach flipped at her agreement—that she wanted to see me after this, that everything I had felt for her was valid, and that I wasn't completely losing my mind as I thought I might be.

Our lips met in a needing manner, her thighs closing on either side of my hips. Her touch lingered on my stubbled cheeks. There was a promise in that kiss. A promise that we would find each other again. That this was not the last time we would see each other.

I crawled onto the bed atop her, making her lay back against the pillows as I hovered there, my now unruly hair falling over my eyes. She held my face, her eyes searching mine.

"What do I do to you?" I asked.

The right corner of her lips quirked—so quickly that had I not been staring at her face, I would have missed it—and she pushed my hair back.

"You make me want to be found."

I couldn't sleep.

Not with all the thoughts of her continuing to run through my mind. I thought about tomorrow, about how facing that day without her suddenly felt empty, perhaps even the worst decision of my life.

This woman.

This… *this fucking woman*….

I opened and closed my phone three times with the intention of changing my flight. I wanted to take her to breakfast, forget work and the numerous meetings I had scheduled just to spend the day with her. Even if it meant sitting on her floor and watching television while she worked.

I would happily do that for her. Stand beside her as she chased all her desires, making sure she felt seen, heard, and touched along the way as she should be.

But I respected her decision not to push, that more wasn't what she wanted. At least not now.

I vowed to find her again.

I closed my phone and held her a little tighter in the hours we had left, formulating what I would do when it came time to leave for the airport. And once I decided, I twisted to hold her against my chest and leaned over to kiss her shoulder.

Tiny freckles dotted her skin there. I counted each and memorized the pattern, pushing her hair back off her neck, my thumb running across her jaw to her bottom lip. She stirred, nuzzling into the pillow slightly and tucking her hands beneath the pillow. Her eyes fluttered open, her lip lifting at the corner, and my own smile rose to meet hers.

"Hey, sexy," she muttered as I brushed her cheek. "Why are you still awake?" she asked in a throaty tone.

"I have to leave soon," I whispered.

"Mmm..." She shuffled closer until she was lying wholly in my arms, and she laid her head on my shoulder to look up at me. "Kiss me until the last second," she said. "Until all I will feel at sunrise is the last of your touch on my skin."

My heart somersaulted with every word. Gods, she was gorgeous. Her bright eyes, the way she stared at me right then, the snow coming down out the window behind her. I took a mental picture of it, knowing I would never see anything as magnetic and wonderful as her lying in my arms again.

"Did you get that from a romance novel?" I asked, and that fucking smile spread wider on her lips.

"You would be surprised how beautiful minotaur erotica can be," she said.

I chuckled softly, pushing her hair behind her ear. "You are so fucking beautiful," I whispered.

Her lips pressed together in a soft smile, another glance of sheepishness like when I'd called her that earlier. But she cleared her throat and laid her head on the pillow, her eyes sparkling at me. "You're not so bad yourself."

I returned her smile before leaning in to kiss her. Tenderly. Savoring her taste and touch for one last time. And when we parted, I wrapped her up, my lips pressing to her nose and her forehead, her cheek and her jaw, her neck and then back to her cheek, making her laughter sing into the still night as she relaxed in my arms once again.

She fit against my chest, my body forming against hers as though it remembered her from a distant memory, a past life. I wasn't sure what it meant, but I didn't spend time thinking about it then, not with the few moments I had left with her.

My eyes began to droop, the comforting way we molded together sending my soul into rest. I fought that sleep, desperate to hang on to whatever time we had left.

I didn't know how to let her go, and I never wanted to.

Chapter Twenty

Chloe

Sunlight poured through the sheer black curtains to my left, casting winter's golden glow over my pillows. I woke up in a haze, my body aching in the best way. I stretched my arms wide, feeling my thighs twitch, and a groan escaped my sore throat. As I rolled over, the remainder of Gavin's peppered scent hit me. The delicious, sweet musk wafted toward me as though it had been sprayed on the fabric. A smile rose on my lips.

It hadn't been a dream.

I could still smell him on my skin, still feel every touch burned onto me like a new tattoo. He had done as I'd asked. He had made me feel as though I belonged to him with all the places he'd kissed me. Every brush of his tongue and touch of his fingers were brands of a night I wished had never ended. I couldn't wait to get up and see all the marks left on my body from our tumble.

My eyes fluttered open to the space he'd laid in the last few hours, and I almost chuckled at what he'd left on my pillow.

There was a note, the red handcuffs, and a candy—one that read SWEET GIRL—and a warmth filled my chest at the sight of it, spreading up my neck to my ears. The paper fell open when I shifted, and the most ridiculous smile I'd ever felt spread on my lips at the scribble in the middle of it.

I'll find you.

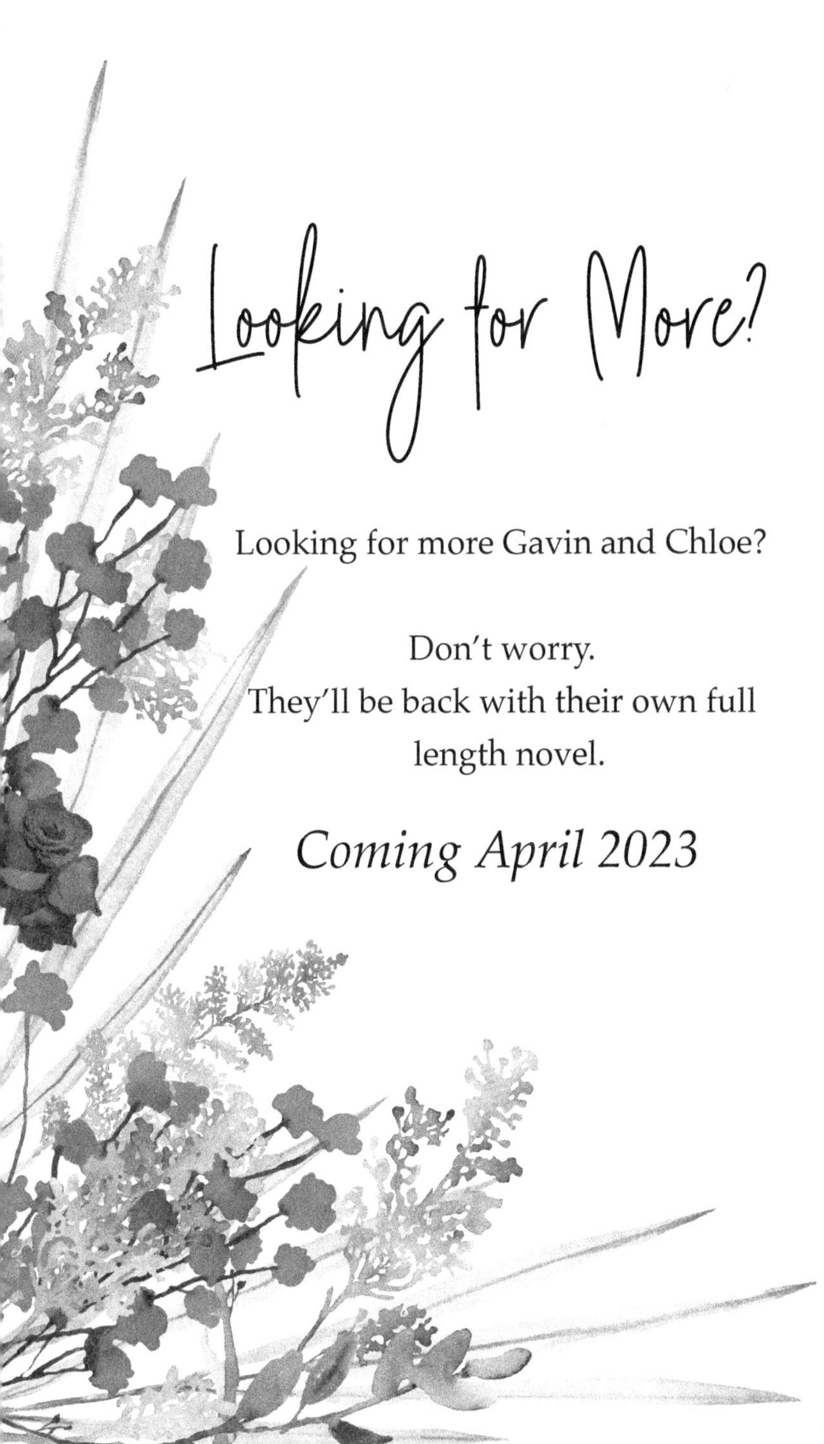

Looking for More?

Looking for more Gavin and Chloe?

Don't worry.
They'll be back with their own full
length novel.

Coming April 2023

Acknowledgments

Ah, acknowledgments…

I just want to say thank you to everyone who made this book what it is and helped me take it to that next level. It blows my mind every time when I look at those orange banners from last year and the wild response it generated from both Booktok and Bookstagram. Thank you for loving Gavin and Chloe as I do. You all are my heroes, and I cannot thank you enough!

To Emily, thank you for squeezing me in last minute for this cover! I absolute love it and YOU! You are amazing.

To Angie, thank you for helping me sort through this to get it to 1st Person POV, and for always being there in general. You are the absolute best, and I could not be more grateful to have you as my editor and as my friend.

To Kay, thank you for always cheering me on and keeping my thoughts organized (because I am scatterbrained as fuck). I wish you were coming with me to StoryBound, but there will be so many more 'next time's'!

As always, I want to thank my amazing street team for being the most awesome people on the planet and helping me with everything. I love y'all.

I am very excited to bring Gavin and Chloe's full novel this April. They have been so much fun to write, and seeing everyone's response to them is just mind-blowing.

And since you've all been *so good*, turn the page ;-) The first three chapters of Finding You are waiting.

Finding You

Chapter One
Chloe

The quad-shot espresso with oat milk in my hand was not enough coffee to start the day.

It had begun with nearly having an argument with my best friend, and then on the way to work, I'd tripped on three cracks in the sidewalk when my heels got caught. It rained on my walk from the parking garage, and I'd dropped my cell phone in a puddle that looked like it had a layer of oil floating on the top. Not to mention I'd barely been able to sleep due to the weird dreams I'd been having. I kept seeing a hill, golden wings, and feeling shadowed hands touching me. No face, just the shadow. What was most bewildering, though, was the feeling I woke up with every time— butterflies in my stomach, heated cheeks, restlessness in my muscles, an aching heart…

"I think I'm dying," I had told my best friend, Lana, that morning on our video chat. Since I'd moved across the country last year, video calls had been our daily ritual. I missed her more than I could express. There was something about Lana that lit up an entire room and made everyone around her feel comfortable. Maybe it was her psychology background, or perhaps it was just Lana's presence. But I could tell her everything, and she could read me like a book.

"That medical site says I'm dying," I continued.

"You can't trust those sites, babe," Lana said, crossing her legs and leaning her elbow onto the countertop. Her black cat jumped on the barstool beside her, and she pulled the feline into her lap. "You put in 'stuffy nose' and it comes back with nasal tumors. How did you say you felt again?"

"Hi, Salem," I cooed to the beautiful little cat. "She's getting big."

"Stop stalling," Lana said. "Let's hear it. How did you feel?"

I twisted the bread bag and wrapped the tie around it before throwing two pieces in the toaster. "Racing— no, aching heart. Weak knees. Like… adrenaline? Dopamine? Almost giddy, as if you've had a glass of red wine—"

"I'd like to know what kind of red wine you're drinking," Lana muttered behind the cup of tea at her lips.

I pursed my lips at her, and she chuckled, her spiraled curls falling out of the colorful headband she had wrapped around her head. "Right. Go on. What else?"

"Ah… Warm. My stomach was fluttering almost—"

"Are you sure you didn't eat anything odd?" Lana asked.

"I've had this same dream for a week now. Multiple times in the past. I don't think it has anything to do with my eating habits," I replied.

"I mean, you did eat an entire large pepperoni pizza by yourself last night," Lana teased.

My lips twisted as I tried to deny a smile, pressing my palms into the edge of the counter. "Tyler is out of town," I argued. "And it was a buffalo chicken pizza—"

"Extra hot sauce, ranch, and a few cider beers," Lana knew. "Did you also have the strawberry ice cream?"

My toast popped up, and I took it out to smear red pepper jelly on it. "Pistachio, actually."

Lana laughed softly and took another drink of her tea, her eyes still sleepy from the caffeine not kicking in yet. "Where's Tyler this week?"

Tyler Drake. My fiancé.

We'd been together three years, engaged for two of them. I'd had the hardest time picking a date—to the point that I'd handed all decisions over to Tyler and my mother. The date, the location, the decor, even my dress.

"Ah… Florida," I said as I sat down at the table with my toast and coffee. "His father wanted to talk to him about the latest investment." I slapped a sarcastic smile on my lips. "It's very exciting."

"Sounds like it," Lana muttered.

Tyler was—what he liked to call—an entrepreneur. He's had his hands in various small business that he swears will be the next big thing, along with owning a few pieces of real estate. He was always traveling to check on things.

"What about the wedding? Three-month countdown, right?" Lana said.

I nodded and took a bite of toast. "Are you coming next week?" I asked.

"For your dress fitting? Wouldn't miss it. Especially since you picked it out without me," Lana replied, batting her lashes and giving me a tight-lipped smile.

"You know I had to do that while my mom was in town—"

"Along with your sisters and Tyler's mom," Lana interjected.

"I'm honestly surprised we found anything. It was the first shop, and you know how particular my sisters are," I finished.

"They all made sure you found something while they were there," Lana said. "And I'm still trying to figure out why they chose your dress and not you."

I chewed my toast, my stomach knotting. "They've chosen everything else. Why not my dress, too?" I asked softly.

"Because it's your fucking wedding—"

"You know I don't care about those things," I argued. "They do."

"And why don't you care about those things?"

Sometimes I hated her.

I sighed and downed the rest of my coffee. "Can we talk about this later?" I said as I stood to clean up the table. "Like… after I've had a few glasses of wine and a big fat steak?"

"Oh, is that what we're having for dinner tonight?"

"It's Friday, and Tyler has some fancy dinner with a client, so I won't hear from him until like two in the morning. Therefore, yes. You're my date, and we're ordering in a three courser. Don't worry, I'll order yours too."

"Such a gentleman," Lana said, giving a kissy face to the screen. "Hey, do you think the bridal boutique will also have my dress in to try on?"

"I'll have Tyler call to make sure they do. He can probably pull a few strings."

Lana scoffed. "You mean slap a few hundred dollars in their hands and demand to be taken care of?"

"You're the only person I know that would say that condescendingly."

"It's not a bad thing," Lana shrugged. "He just throws money at any problem he might come across. Including any problem with you."

"Lana…" And I said her name in a warning tone, my jaw tightening. It was too early for this conversation, too early to hear her complain about Tyler or bring up any qualms she might have with or about him.

"I'm just saying… Maybe these dreams you're having are part of the universe's way of talking to you," Lana said.

My mouth twisted in annoyance. "What?"

"The things you're describing sound like what it feels like to realize you're in love," she continued. "The warmth. The aching heart, butterflies in your stomach, restless muscles, dopamine, weak knees… Maybe it's your soul reaching out."

"Reaching out for what?" I asked in disbelief.

"For its counterpart," Lana said.

I huffed as I rinsed my cup out. "You're ridiculous."

"Am I, though?" Lana asked.

A heavy sigh left me. I was engaged. I didn't know what she was saying. I knew she didn't like Tyler all that much, but this?

"I have to stop by the coffee shop for espresso," I said. "Barely got any sleep."

"Because you were banging that shadow all night," Lana said with a wink. "I'm telling you, babe. The universe is speaking to you. Your soul is crying out and trying to tell you something."

"That I'm dying and having hot flashes?"

Lana scoffed. "You should listen to it."

"Lana…"

"I know, I know—"

"It's not that I don't believe in that kind of thing," I said quickly. "I just… I like where life is right now. I'm not exactly looking for something to come in and change all of that."

"That's a lovely comfort zone you're treading in," Lana mocked.

"Goodbye, Lana," I said in a sing-song voice.

Lana grinned. "Talk to you tonight, babe."

Thank fuck, it was Friday.

I'd thought about everything Lana had said the entire way to my office—which was probably why I'd nearly broken my ankle on the sidewalk.

At least judging by the others in the office elevator, I was not the only person with a shit morning. Everyone was wet and clutching coffees like that was our jobs, not the ones we were heading to. My new marketing firm was on the thirteenth and fourteenth floors of a large building. I'd founded it with a friend just before meeting Tyler three years ago. We'd started out small, taking on a couple of my clients that I already had and bringing them in for full projects rather than just a few ads like I had been delivering.

Things were going really well, and since moving to California the year before and adding this new office space and a cluster of employees, we'd grown exponentially, even landing a few more prominent clients.

Jasmine, my assistant, met me as the elevator doors opened on the fourteenth floor. I frowned at her standing there looking antsy and excited with a grin on her face, and clenching her hands together in front of her.

"Morning, Jasmine," I said upon reaching her.

"Good morning," she replied in a chipper voice.

"What's happening?" I asked. "You never meet me at the doors."

"Did you not get the email this morning?" she asked.

I took a sip of my coffee—my too-hot coffee—and grimaced at the way it burned my mouth. "I've made it a rule never to check my email before the start of a workday," I told her. I'd started too many mornings already stressed out by checking email, and had chosen a few years back to protect my sanity by holding off until logging in.

"Why?" I batted away a heart balloon that someone walking past was carrying. "What did I miss?"

"New client," Jasmine said as she plucked a rose from one of the tables and smelled it. "Ezzie is going around ordering decorations already to celebrate."

Another heart balloon came into my sight line, and I started to realize they were everywhere. And the moment we rounded the corner, I stopped in my tracks.

Hearts—large red hearts—in balloon form hovered all around the open workspace. There were pink, white, and red confetti hearts on all the tables, streamers on the doors, pink heart pillows on the community couches, and some of our poufs had been replaced by red floor pillows.

I couldn't stop staring at the audacious decor. "Did someone get engaged?" I asked.

"Ezzie thought it was fitting," Jasmine said.

"It is *May*," I said, completely flabbergasted that there was heart decor everywhere. "What the shitbox," I muttered. We continued walking to the back of the room where my office was. "Who is the client?"

The phone on Jasmine's desk rang before she couldn't answer. She slipped away quickly to answer it, and I strode inside my office, tossing my bag onto the chair by the door. Red roses decorated my desk in a tall white vase, no card or indication as to who they were from. Though, the more I thought about it, I realized maybe they were just part of Ezzie's decor.

I wracked my brain trying to figure out who she had landed for her to be changing the office over to red and pink instead of our signature black and green.

There was an email with the subject line 'NEW CLIENT BITCH' at the top of the priorities folder on my computer. I took a moment to settle in my chair before opening it, and when I did, my entire body froze at the logo in the middle of the email.

My heart skipped, heat suddenly beating on my cheeks. I felt like someone was lighting a fire to my entire being. Visions of hands, hearts, snow, and sweating flesh flashed through my mind. Candy hearts on my tongue, a hand across my ass, the noise of cursing to the gods.

"That's my good girl."

The memory of that rasping voice sent a shiver down my spine.

"Oh, fucking hell," I muttered.

Jasmine knocked on the doorframe, making me flinch. "Dani wants to know if you have time to look over the Halloween campaign she's working on."

The email had me off-kilter. All noise around me muted.

Cupid's fucking Arrow.

The dating app, Cupid's Arrow, was our newest client.

Fuck. Fuck. *Fuck.*

It continued to be the most popular dating app out there, even after the influx of other dating apps trying to emulate their algorithm. Cupid's Arrow had an advantage over the others though that no one knew about.

It was founded by the god of lust himself.

Eros.

He was parading around as a mortal named Gavin Erosin. As for how long he'd been in this disguise, I wasn't sure. I hadn't seen him since that Valentine's Day party five years ago—a night I thought about more often than I should have.

I didn't bother reading the remainder of the project description. All I could think about was Gavin. I hadn't felt like that since then. I hadn't felt that kind of desire, lust, or absolute greed for another person. The thought of seeing him again… It knotted and twisted everything in me to the point that I was nauseous.

It wasn't that I didn't want to see him—because fuck, I did.

It was that seeing him scared the shit out of me.

I wondered how I would feel now that I was engaged to someone else. I wondered if that need would still be there. It was only one night, but it had been a night of more than just wild sex. We had truly connected, and by the time the sun rose, I could see myself actually being in a relationship with him. I had felt genuine laughter, want, and happiness that night which I hadn't thought possible with someone who I also had an intimate relationship. I'd even opened up with him about my father and my past—something I never did.

We had parted ways and returned to our normal lives the next day with no way of reaching the other.

I'd often thought about if I'd made a mistake not asking him to change flights the next morning.

"Hello?" Jasmine called. "Earth to Chloe."

I snapped out of my daze, blinking myself back to reality. "Yeah, sorry, what did you ask?"

"Dani wants to know if you have time to look at the project she's on," Jasmine repeated.

"Ah… Actually—" I gathered my things and started to stand. "Actually, I need to go talk to Ezzie about the email. I'll… Tell Dani to email it to me and I'll look at it today."

"Are you okay?" Jasmine asked.

"Yeah. I'm fine. I'll be back after lunch."

And I left my office without another word.

I had to see Ezzie to find out more details.

As I entered the elevator, I took my phone out and sent a text to Lana.

Make sure you bring vodka to our date tonight. You'll need it, I sent.

It's barely nine and you already need vodka?

We have a new client.

Oh? Tell me more.

You use it on the daily.

Toilet paper?

I snorted. No. *An app. A dating app.*

Three dots strummed at the bottom of my screen for as long as it took me on the elevator and to cross the room to Ezzie's office. I had just closed the phone when Lana's text came through, and I tapped my screen to see it.

You shut your fucking mouth right now

Ezzie's office was on the thirteenth floor. We had the same office, just one floor apart. The same corner, the same size, but Ezzie was on the business floor while I ran the creative floor.

Ez was pacing back and forth, EarPods in and talking on the phone when I reached her. I knew which client she was talking to without needing an explanation. Ez's negotiating skills was one of the reasons we'd gone into business together. I would handle the creative side, and she could handle the business side.

Though taking on the most popular dating app out there was not exactly what I'd had in mind.

Babe! I need details! Lana was texting.

Did you see him?

Is he still hot?

I shook my head and crossed my hands in front of me as I waited on Ez. She glanced sideways and finally saw me. Her face lit up, and she held up a finger, signaling me to wait to talk to her.

I looked down at my phone one more time, finding that Lana had sent one more message.

Look at the universe, and there was a wink-face emoji after the words.

I resisted throwing my phone and instead opened it up just as Ez was hanging up her own phone call.

I hate you.

Love youuuuu, she said with a kissy-face

"Chloe!" Ezzie said enthusiastically, her arms in the air, and I realized she had finally hung up her phone. I snapped my attention to her and placed my phone in the back pocket of my dark jeans.

Ezzie's beautiful face was glowing. Her short, dark blue hair was lightly curled today, a nude color on her plump lips, and light, simple makeup that accentuated her amber skin. I was envious of her style. Today's outfit consisted of high-waisted black pants with small, vertical white stripes and a snug black long-sleeve top that fit her arms, full breasts, and stopped around her ribs, showing off her soft mid-drift.

And barefoot, as she always was around the office.

Ezzie was a tall, plus-size goddess who commanded attention. When she, Lana, myself, and Ezzie's girlfriend, Raegan, went to dinner or a bar, it was hard to contain us. Tyler had even made a point in the past to take himself out of town to his parents' when Lana and Raegan were visiting.

"Morning, Ez," I said, wishing I could return her enthusiasm.

"Anything you'd like to tell me?" Ezzie grinned, folding her arms over her chest and lifting up her chin. "Anything like 'you're the best' or 'congratulations on nailing that contract, you fucking goddess' or—"

"Great job, you fucking divine ," I said with a small clap, chuckling at how proud she was.

She flipped her hair off her shoulders and did a slight bow. "Thank you, thank you. Actually, it was pretty easy. They contacted us," she said with a laugh.

"Who contacted you?" I asked.

"It was…" Ezzie leaned over her desk and clicked a few times on her computer. "Avril Patel," she finally said. "She's over their marketing department. Says she wants to do a special campaign, including new logos, for their tenth anniversary, and she's having trouble hiring new staff so she decided to outsource since it was such a large project."

I let the sentence sink in and took a deep breath, putting on my logical face and ignoring the emotional side that was screaming.

"So, when do we start?" I asked. "Who is our contact? Are we meeting in person or—"

"Are you okay?" Ezzie cut in.

I balked. "Yeah. Why?"

"Your vibe is off," she said. "What's wrong? You're normally excited about new projects, especially large ones with well-known clients."

"I'm excited."

"Tell your face," Ezzie said with a raised brow.

My lips pursed and I looked at the ground. I couldn't hide anything from Ezzie. She always saw through my facade when something was wrong.

"Wedding things," I only halfway lied.

"Ah," Ezzie said, nodding. "Four months out?"

"Lovely August wedding," I said, my tone dripping with sarcasm as I gave her a tight-lipped smile. "I'll be wearing sweat cloths between my thighs."

Ezzie smirked at me. "If I recall, you couldn't choose a date so you let Tyler choose."

I flopped in one of her chairs and sighed. "You sound like Lana," I said.

"Oh, love her. When is she coming?" Ezzie asked.

"She'll be in on Thursday night," I answered. "Remember, I'm taking next week off."

"Perfect timing. I'll try not to bother you. However, we are having a little meet and greet social with some of the team from Cupid's Arrow next Friday. I'd like you to be there to meet everyone."

I nearly hurled on her fluffy white rug, but I knew there was no getting out of it. "Great. Tyler and Lana will be here."

"I'm sure he'll love that," Ezzie teased.

"Yeah," I scoffed. "He will." I slapped the arms of the chair and stood again. "Anything else I should know? I'm going to get a wrap on my other projects before diving into the Cupid's Arrow one."

Or possibly drown myself in nerves and agony.

Whichever came first.

Chapter Two

Gavin

"No, Mother. I am not coming home next week," I said into the phone.

"Oh, but Eros, it's such a special day," my mother cooed.

My brows narrowed as I reached for my coffee off the shop counter. "What's so special?" I asked. The cute barista caught my eye, and I mouthed a quick 'thank you' to her, winking in response to her leer, before turning on my heel toward the door.

"Because I'll be home too, and what's more special than getting to see your own mother?" she replied.

I nearly stopped walking, my face going into a flat expression at her words. "I have work," I said.

"I don't understand *why* you work, love," she said. "It's not like you need to."

"I'm hanging up now," I told her.

"You've done enough mischievous deeds in your life. You could take a step back—"

"So says Aphrodite," I muttered.

"—you don't need the added stress," she continued. "You could come home. Retire. Find a few mortals to bring with—"

"Goodbye, Mother."

I hung up the phone before she could continue. Fucking Styx. I hadn't been home in over a century, and I didn't plan on going any time soon. I enjoyed living a normal life, having a regular job and regular friends. I may have been the god of lust, but that didn't mean I needed to only surround myself with other gods.

I rounded the corner and pushed the revolving door into Cupid's Arrow's headquarters. What had started out as a few desks in an otherwise empty corner building had turned into five open stories of humming workers. No boring cubicles but rather couches and private rooms for projects, floor seats and standing desks, treadmills and rest areas, and so much more. I wanted the environment to nourish productivity rather than box it in, and my team had delivered on that.

Of course, the arrows and hearts theme had grown a bit out of control over the years. It was one of the reasons why I requested a logo overhaul and rebrand for our tenth anniversary.

The building was already in a buzz as I entered and pushed my shades up atop my head. A few friends greeted me with words or handshakes. I made my way up to the fifth floor, phone out and checking on numbers. I was consumed with the numbers and loved the gratification of seeing the number of new users and interactions every day.

For a few hours every day, I toyed with the matches. Some for good, some for fun. I checked in on some throughout the week just to see how things were going, and loved it when things went completely sideways, or when matches that shouldn't have made it, actually worked out. I'd been to a few of those weddings, carrying an arrow with me just in case things needed a final nudge.

Avril, my marketing director, was waiting for me at the top of the stairs. A middle-aged woman who could run circles around any of the younger techs there. She was my right hand at the company, my go-to person who I could count on to carry out any wild ideas I might have. She was one of the first people I hired in the early days—just arriving from India with her family and looking for work. Her background was in event work and sales, and there was just something about her that I loved. She had become family over the years. I'd lost track of how many holidays I'd spent visiting her house for dinners.

"Good morning, Cupid," she said in her usual teasing tone.

I kissed her cheek as I hit the top step. "Morning, Av. What's new?" I asked, continuing to walk.

Avril joined me. "I had Maddi clear your calendar tomorrow evening," she said.

"Why?"

"Social with the company I hired for our ten-year campaign and rebrand."

I paused in my step and looked at her. "We sourced out?"

Avril glanced around us nervously and then nodded to my office. I followed her cue and waited until she had closed the door behind us to continue talking.

"What's up?" I asked.

"Our branding team is short four people," she started. "I hired out because the ones left are spread so thin right now with other projects, I didn't want to overwhelm them. Adding this might push someone into doing work in their downtime."

"I don't want that," I said. Work-life balance had always been important for me. I never wanted anyone working more than they should.

"I know you don't," she said. "Which is why I found another firm to handle it. It'll be nice to have fresh eyes on everything, too. They're a younger company, very eager. I think you'll like them."

"What's their company name?"

"Designare Fusion."

I had never heard of it, but I trusted Avril enough to let her do what she thought was best for the company. "Okay," I said, reaching for a licorice rope out of my candy vase to chew on. "What else should I know about them?"

"Women-owned," she said. "They haven't had an account as large as ours before. I'm interested to see what they make of it. Both owners will be heading up the project."

"The owners actually know how to do work in their field?" I asked.

"One is a marketing and PR guru who was freelancing in public relations to C-list celebrities before this company and working damage control for a few Twitter fiascos. I think she still does a little of that on the side, so should you ever be involved in some tabloid scandal, we have someone to call," she said with a raise of her brow.

My smirk widened. "I'll try to keep my name out of the tabloids just for you," I said. "What about the design aspect?"

"Their designer also worked in freelance graphic design on her own for small, independent companies. She moved from simple Instagram and Facebook posts to designing entire campaigns within a year of going out on her own. Apparently her load became so much that she reached out to Ezra to partner for their own marketing company."

"Ezra?"

"They call her Ezzie. You'll meet her tomorrow."

"What's her partner's name?"

"Ah…" Avril strummed her fingers across the back of the chair she was leaning against. "I can't remember off the top of my head. I'll try to put together a brief for you today, so you don't look so much like one of those incompetent owners tomorrow night."

"You know that's my favorite look," I said.

Avril cocked a brow, her head tilting sideways. "It's not mine, so we're going with what I think."

"Right," I smiled. "Anything else?"

"These people won't be used to working with you, so I need you to somehow figure out a way to represent what you're looking for with the rebrand. I know you're used to throwing ideas off of us like pennies, but with this group—"

"I'll try to get my scatterbrain under control," I said as I sat. I gave her a charming smile and leaned back, to which she rolled her eyes and threw a pen at my face.

"Elliot has paperwork for you to sign," she said before turning toward the door. "I'll tell him to bring them in in an hour."

"Thanks, Av. Go ahead and tell Maddi to take the day off since you're doing her job," I teased.

She paused at the door and batted her lashes sarcastically at me. "Just taking care of my favorite dickhead," she said sweetly.

I adjusted in my seat. "Jeez. I thought your husband's dickhead would be your favorite," I grinned.

Avril threw a pillow from the couch at my head, and I dodged it easily. She was still shaking her head when she closed my glass door.

My phone vibrated. I turned it over, finding a message from my mother on the screen, prompting me to press my elbows into the desk and rub my eyes. She'd been on me about going home for a few years now, and I wasn't sure how long I could keep putting it off. Between that and the little sleep I'd been getting lately, I was exhausted.

I'd started having dreams again—dreams of a feeling and a touch I thought lost forever. In every dream, complete darkness surrounded me and the woman I laid in bed with. I could taste her, smell her, feel her. And every time I had the dream, I only thought of one person: the woman I'd searched for for five years, and found nothing on.

Chloe.

The only regret I had in my life was leaving her.

I still thought about that night almost every day. It drove me crazy that I'd not changed my flight and taken at least the next day with her. I had no way of knowing where she was any longer. She'd deleted the Cupid's Arrow app almost immediately after that Valentine's night, and I hadn't even been smart enough to remember her last name.

I'd nearly gone home just to seek the Oracle about finding her, but I knew better than to think Apollo would ever give me an answer after the way we'd ended things.

I smiled at that memory. *Idiot*. A few friends had told me to apologize for humiliating him so long ago, but the rage on his face when we would randomly see each other over the years was much more fun. I'd even played a few more tricks on him with mortals I knew he was lusting after, sending the same blunted arrows after them so they might despise him as Daphne had.

I chuckled and opened the Cupid's Arrow app on my phone. It was really ignorant of him to use my app in the first place, so why not have a little fun?

Maybe I could even dig up a little dirt on anyone from Designare Fusion while I was on it.

Chapter Three

Chloe

Lana's arrival the next week was a whirlwind of screams and hugs. I hadn't seen her in person in over a year. We'd both been so busy with work that our vacations hadn't lined up. She had planned out our evening already—a whiskey distillery, a nice Thai restaurant, followed by a late night pajama party that Tyler wasn't invited to. He'd chosen to stay with his parents another day to avoid having to stay on the other side of the apartment.

"Fuck all, I can't wait for tomorrow," Lana said as she lounged back in the booth we had picked out at the restaurant. "It's going to be epic."

"I think I'll stay wasted the rest of the week," I muttered against my wine glass. "Champagne tomorrow morning at the fitting. Vodka tomorrow night to get through possibly seeing the god of lust in the same room as my fiancé—"

"Bloody Mary's Saturday morning for the hangover," Lana interjected.

"—Wine that afternoon for dinner with the in-laws," I added.

"Ugh," Lana grunted. "I can't believe you're subjecting me to that torture."

"You can rag on me and complain all you want the next day with mimosas at brunch with the girls," I said.

"Fucking, yes," Lana said. "Can't wait to see Ezzie and Raegan so we can all dish about your little conundrum."

"There is no conundrum," I argued. "One look at Gavin is not going to make me leave Tyler and jump into bed with him," I said.

"Not unless he brings one of his little love arrows," she replied. "Still, it will be fun to fill them in on the details."

I could only imagine the absolute chaos that would ensue once they found out.

Lana and I laughed and chatted all through our dinner, and by the time we headed home, both of us were full on Thai food and on the verge of a drunken stupor. We stopped by a late-night bakery to fuel our slumber party with cheesecake and chocolate before surrendering back to my apartment.

"—until you see the onesie I found," Lana said as we exited the elevator to my floor. "It's my favorite animal."

"Unicorn or narwhal?" I asked. I fumbled for my keys, almost tripping on the rug down the hallway.

"Aren't they—*oh shit!*" Lana grabbed me to keep from falling—unsuccessfully, and both of us burst into laughter, cursing and sinking to the floor in our dresses.

Our cackles moved down the hall, so loud that one of my neighbors came to their door to check and see if we were okay, which sent us into hysterics.

I forced myself to my knees and pushed the key into the lock. We fell onto the floor when the door opened, and for a few moments, both of us had to lean against the walls to collect ourselves.

"We shouldn't have had that last champagne," Lana laughed.

"*You* shouldn't have had that last champagne," I joked.

"You're so toasted," Lana replied.

"It looks like you both are," came a familiar voice.

My laugh fell so quickly that I started choking.

Tyler was home.

He was standing by the bar pouring white wine into the three glasses he had sat out atop it. Only the amber globe lights were on above the counter, casting shadows across his trimmed, dark brown wavy hair and fading over his pale face. He must have cut it while he was seeing his parents—probably his mother said something to him about it looking untidy.

A bouquet of roses and a small box sat beside the wine glasses.

"Tyler," I managed, gathering my wits and catching my breath. "Tyler, I didn't think you would be home."

His dark brows narrowed slightly, a smirk on his thin lips. "You sound disappointed," he said.

"What—no." I tripped on my heels again as I stood, my drunkenness showing in the stammer. "No, I just… I thought you were still in Florida," I said once I'd made it to my feet.

I tried to force myself sober.

Though, it failed spectacularly.

"Hey," I said upon reaching him. He wrapped a hand around my waist and kissed me, and I pushed my hand through his wavy hair. A quiet moan sounded from him, and when he pulled back, he gazed at me with narrow eyes.

"You're so drunk," he said. "I can taste the vodka on your breath."

"I know how much you love vodka," I said, knowing it was his least favorite. "Hence why I drank it when I thought you were away."

He chuckled under his breath, his dark eyes moving toward the door. "Hi, Lana," he said, and I could feel his body tense as he spoke to her.

Lana's happy expression had faded, replaced with a fake smile that I knew all too well. "Tyler," she said, stalking our way. "Fancy seeing you here a day early."

"Couldn't have you stealing my girl away, could I?" he said, his hand tightening on me.

"Doubt I'd have to steal her," she said as she grabbed one of the glasses of wine he'd poured. "She'd come willingly."

"Play nice," I said, hitting Tyler's chest gently. "Both of you," I added with a glance at Lana.

She grinned coyly and batted her lashes at Tyler, then looked at me. "Only for you, babe," she said. "So, Tyler, will you be joining our pajama party?"

"I'll take a pass," he said. "I need to catch up on a couple of emails and get to sleep. I spent most of the day in the airport."

"Oh, you poor thing," Lana mocked with a pout.

I peered over his shoulder then, truly noticing the roses and the box on the counter. I'd been in such a daze five minutes earlier that I saw it and forgot about it that quickly. "What's this?" I asked.

"Ah…" He released me, and I smelled one of the roses while he pushed the box in my direction.

"Open it," he said.

I knew what the long box was before I even opened the lid. A diamond bracelet. I picked it up out of the box and held it carefully in my hands.

"My mother said it would go well with your dress. Don't worry, she didn't show it to me," he assured me.

An emptiness settled in my stomach as I stared. I wasn't used to expensive and shiny things like this, yet Tyler insisted on buying it for me again and again. I felt awkward wearing such extravagance. I had even been awkward about the enormous ring he'd given me. I appreciated the gesture more than I could say, but I knew I wouldn't wear expensive jewelry and spending money on it wasn't something I wanted him to do. "Wow," Lana said over my shoulder. "Look at that."

Sarcasm dripped in her tone.

"It's beautiful," I forced out. "But you know you didn't have to," I said, meeting his eyes.

"I know. I was told I should wait until our wedding day to give it to you. Something about a gift exchange tradition? But I wanted to give it to you now. I've been away a lot this month on this project. I wanted to make it up to you."

Was it horrible that I hadn't noticed his hardly being home over the last month?

"It's fine," I said. "I love it."

A lie, but I was too tipsy to get into it then, and with Lana there, the argument would have been over the top.

Tyler leaned in and kissed my cheek before taking the box out of my hands. "I'll put this away somewhere safe," he said. "I'm off to bed. Wake me when you come in?"

I nodded, trying to keep the forced smile on my face and not let my expression betray me. He kissed me again, then headed toward the bedroom.

"Night, Lana," he said as he passed.

"We'll try to keep it down," Lana said, her voice dripping with a smart-aleck flare.

The moment he disappeared into the bedroom and we heard the door snap closed, Lana looked at me with an expectant glare.

"Not a word," I said, grabbing my wine.

Lana's lips pressed together thinly, and I could tell it was taking everything in her to bite back the words on her tongue. I knew she wanted to say something about his being there, about the gift he'd bought that even she knew I wouldn't like, and most especially, about my poor attempt to sober up upon seeing him.

"Narwhal," I said firmly.

Lana huffed. "Fine. But we're talking about it tomorrow."

Tomorrow.

Fucking hell, *tomorrow.*

I downed my wine at the thought of what was possibly happening the next day, Gavin's face flashing behind my eyes, and my stomach flipped.

One thing at a time, Chloe, I reminded myself.

Coming Soon

I hope you enjoyed that little sneak
peek. Stay tuned for their entire book,
Finding You,
coming in April 2023.

Other Works by Jack Whitney

DEAD MOONS RISING
BOOK ONE IN THE HONEST SCROLLS SERIES

FLAMES OF PROMISE
BOOK TWO IN THE HONEST SCROLLS SERIES

THE GATHERING
AN HONEST SCROLLS NOVELLA

SWEET GIRL
A CUPID NOVELLA

BALLAD OF NIGHTMARES
BOOK ONE IN THE NIGHTMARES DUOLOGY

ANYONE AND YOU
AN AUTUMN EROTICA NOVELLA

BREAK THE GLASS
A HALLOWEEN EROTICA NOVELLA

COMING SOON IN 2023:

FINDING YOU
A SWEET GIRL NOVEL
APRIL 2023

About The Author

Jack Whitney is an adult dark fantasy and romance author out of
North Carolina, US.
You can usually find her playing in dark and strange worlds.
Her characters are always in charge.
She is fueled by coffee, whiskey, and shadow daydreams.
If you're reading her books, they probably came with a warning
label.

Welcome to the Nightmare of Ravens.

Jack also feels very weird about writing bios because
she's not sure what you want to know.
She is almost always stalking social media and procrastinating, so
if you would like to find her to ask more questions, please feel
free.

@Jack.Whitney.Writer

9 7 9 8 9 8 5 5 0 8 8 6 4